On Bolton Flats

AN IRISH INSURRECTION IN VERMONT'S NORTH WOODS

J. Peter Konkle

Based on the true story of two hundred desperate Irish families fleeing the Potato Famine and recruited with unfulfilled promises to build an ill-fated section of the Vermont Central Railroad.

On Bolton Flats
An Irish Insurrection In Vermont's North Woods

Front cover photo and other historical documents provided by and published with the permission of the Vermont Historical Society, Montpelier, Vermont, and the Vermont History Library, Barre, Vermont.

For information on educational discounts or bulk purchases, please contact the author.

A Teacher's Guide is available by contacting: jpkonkle@gmail.com.

ISBN-13: 9781493574346
ISBN-10: 1493574345

ACKNOWLEDGEMENTS

Thank you to William (Bill) Kemsley, Sr., now deceased, former United Auto Workers Union member and officer, former President of the Vermont Labor History Society, and former member of the Vermont Labor Relations Board, who encouraged this author to become interested in Vermont's labor history. Thank you, also, to the Vermont Historical Society and the Vermont History Library for keeping the records and ephemera so often and easily lost to time and neglect.

On Bolton Flats

AN IRISH INSURRECTION IN VERMONT'S NORTH WOODS

FORWARD

This is a fictionalized re-telling of an actual event known in Vermont as "The Bolton War". It was not an actual war, but rather an act of civil disobedience culminating in a work stoppage and demonstration by immigrant construction workers protesting a number of significant grievances typical of the era. In late winter, 1846, two hundred Irish workers, fleeing a severe potato famine and centuries of oppression by their British occupiers, were recruited out of Canada by the Vermont Central Railroad Company with unfulfilled promises of food, shelter, and wages in exchange for their labor.

Recruits were housed in a mud-encrusted valley, and the promised wages were never received. The "Burlington Free Press" at the time reported that sixteen to eighteen workers were killed during the first three months of the construction season, adding to the list of the workers' grievances, and leaving new widows and orphans to fend for themselves in a strange new world. The fact that the exact number of work-related deaths was not officially recorded is an indication of the immigrants' low status and the lack of regulation of economic activities far from industrial centers.

A five acre field known locally as "Bolton Flats" lies west of Waterbury, Vermont, and is located at mile marker 69 on Interstate I-89 in central Vermont. Pinneo Brook cascades down the west side of an escarpment that forms the eastern boundary of the flood plain. Forests border the north and west, and the Winooski River, formerly known as the Onion River, lays to the south. A single dirt road was the only connection from Montpelier, the state capitol, west to the City of Burlington on Lake Champlain and the several towns in between, including Jonesville and Richmond. The workers' two camps, named Dublin and Cork by the workers, were located on the floodplain on the north side of the Winooski, and separated by a small rocky outcropping in the center of the Field.

The goal for the 1846 construction season for this crew was to lay five miles of track from east to west. The business environment of the day was virtually free of regulation and government oversight, and the VCRR was competing with another railroad coming up the Champlain Valley to reach the riches of Canada's natural resources. That competition added to the pressure on the company's decision-makers to lay track as fast as possible and to keep costs to an absolute minimum.

Periodically, potato blights blackened the crops that sustained the Irish. However, by the early 1840's, there were no food stores to draw on, and crop failures were so pervasive that grass, tree bark, and even leather shoes were eaten for sustenance. Rumors persisted that the most desperate had resorted to cannibalism. British rule and their inheritance laws had forced land-owning native Irish, over time, into servitude and to become tenant farmers for their British overlords. Hundreds of thousands of families were forced off their ancestors' land in pursuit of survival while thousands more died where they lived following each year's crop failure. Many who were able boarded ships for passage to North America, most not knowing their fate once they landed.

By 1846 there was well-established commerce between North America and Europe, so ships that brought goods and raw materials from Canada and New England to the British Isles, accepted passengers for their return trips. But these ships were not designed to carry human cargo, and given the weakened state of most of the passengers, the death and disease accompanying each voyage caused these vessels to be called "Coffin Ships". The dead were simply dumped over the rail and into the ocean without ceremony.

To add to the desperation felt by the immigrants most had paid a British agent in Ireland for passage to North America and a promise that they would be met at their destination by someone who would help them settle in their new country. Not surprisingly, there was no such help when they disembarked, so they readily accepted any offer of work, and the railroads were there to recruit the labor they needed.

A young woman, Catherine Driscoll Dillon, and her husband were earlier immigrants to Central Vermont. They built and ran a boarding-house and tavern each season near the construction crews and followed the crews as they advanced westward toward Burlington. By the time the railroad reached Rouses Point, Vermont, Catherine was quite wealthy, in part by smuggling untaxed liquor from Canada in order to avoid the United States' restrictions on the import and sale of alcohol. Her obituary, printed in its entirety in the postscript, describes how Catherine bribed officials when necessary in order to avoid arrest and confinement. Mrs. Dillon also secured a permanent separation from her husband by orchestrating a scheme re-told in this account, however, she actually executed her plan several years later than is depicted here. Her obituary is re-printed in the postscript and reads, in part:

> *"She kept a boarding house for the laborers along the line of the roads as they progressed to Rouses Point. At her boarding house, whiskey was always to be obtained by her boarders and others in spite of the contractors."*

Railroad management was hostile to Mrs. Dillon because they felt the liquor she provided reduced worker productivity. Perhaps more importantly, she was a constant symbol of a freer life. Workers and their families recruited to an isolated work site with unfulfilled promises were easier to control, and less likely to escape before their servitude was satis-fied, if they could see no way out.

The nearest law officer, Sheriff Ferris, worked out of Richmond, Vermont, and often did the bidding of the railroad. The railroad didn't like Catherine making liquor available to the immigrant workers, so the Sheriff made life for Catherine more difficult.

Buckboards, stagecoaches, and people on horseback traveled the Stage Road daily, but it was still wilderness; a hour's rough ride to the nearest doctor, and five miles to the nearest hotel, post office, and gen-eral store in Jonesville. Trapped by distance and desperation in a com-pany town of tents pitched on a muddy field, the Irish were the 19th century's chain gangs of industry doing what they were told, and doing what they must to survive.

Chapter 1

HEAR NO EVIL

Belknap thinks I'm deaf. Twenty-two pounds of dynamite evaporated three men, blew apart two more, and left me on my back, unconscious, and bleeding from my nose and ears. The managers put me in a tent with the other injured men and one very unlucky dog to recover or die. The retriever survived because he was close to the ground, and I survived because the hulk of a man I was following stood between me and the blast. Being just an inch or two taller than five feet, what I lack in height I make up for in guile. The dog and I survived because we were the lowest to the ground and lowest in the pecking order.

I remained deaf for the rest of the 1845 construction season, and it seemed like a death sentence at the time. Couldn't hear a damned thing. If I hadn't had a broken shoulder and dizzy spells the bosses would have put me right back to work cutting timber, laying the rail bed or, worst yet, blasting rock. But, I made myself useful for the rest of the season in other ways, and as it turned out, having a deaf butler came in handy in the backwoods of Vermont; a little bit of luxury for bottom-of-the-rung railroad management overseeing half-starved Irish families camped in tent cities set down north of nowhere.

I've seen 'em send an entire family packing when the man got hurt. A man would be let go if he couldn't lift a shovel, move stone, or swing a broad axe, in which case he was of no use to the company. If he didn't owe the company any money they'd put him on a supply train making the round trip from Northfield. If he did owe 'em money and couldn't work, the poor bloke could pay what he owes the company store or

1

they'd take what they wanted from his meager possessions before they put him out by the Stage Road to fend for himself. Widows, children — didn't matter. Some chose to walk the Stage Road to Jonesville five miles west, then on to Richmond, and some continued on another ten miles more to Burlington or to Winooski where factory work might be found.

They'd think nothing of getting rid of a widower like me, 'cept I didn't have a family to feed, and they knew I didn't drink all that much, and if I did, I was always ready to work the next day. Turns out having both ears drums burst probably saved my life. Almost immediately the supervisors put me to work doing housekeeping chores. The dog stayed on, too.

People started calling him "Lucky." Before the accident he used to go hunting and retrieve the game the supervisors shot. Since the accident, Lucky gets spooked when he hears a gunshot or any loud bang. Now, instead of running toward the game, he runs toward the shooter, drops to his belly, and starts barking. He doesn't stop for four or five minutes. Not much use as a retriever.

These days, instead of earning his keep as a retriever, Lucky chases away varmints from the supply sheds during the construction season, and is a pet to Mrs. Dillon during the winter. Mrs. Dillon runs what she calls a boardinghouse, but she makes more money from whiskey than boarders.

So I took a lesson from Lucky. Instead of me laboring in the cold rain or blistering sun laying track, I'm now a gentleman's gentleman in the North woods. While the other workers eat beans and cornbread, Lucky and I eat meat, potatoes, and greens — good food even if they're just leftovers from the supervisors' table. Here's a life lesson: Sometimes what at first appears to be a misfortune, can be a blessing. Ya might say, and I would if I chose to speak, I was blessed with a misfortune.

The accident was described in the Burlington newspaper as a "premature detonation" with no mention of the casualties. Casualties were a presumption, a foregone conclusion, when constructing railroads, particularly through the mountains of northern New England. The railroad barons in Massachusetts and Connecticut were fortunate that millions of Irish were starving to death under the thumb of the Brits across the sea. The Potato Famine in the early '40's was the worst yet - bad enough to force whole families, or what was left of them, to escape their ancestral homes because there was simply nothing to eat. The famines were becoming more frequent and more devastating; the black fungus spread over a wider area of Ireland and the British Isles with each passing year.

The winter months in Ireland took more and more lives as everything that could be chewed and swallowed disappeared, including grass and discarded shoe leather. The livestock and horses were eaten early on; then dogs and cats followed by mice and rats. Men put on harnesses meant for lowly beasts of burden, to haul their belongings to the coast and onto ships bound for North America.

The Famine in Ireland made for an unlimited supply of eager workers with the right attitude: they'd do anything to simply survive, and that's good for business – particularly for North America's new railroad industry. Near the end of last year's construction season my hearing started to come back, but I didn't let on for fear that I would lose my new job. By then, you see, I had become invisible. I was invisible because I was deaf. I didn't say anything for weeks after the accident so they thought I was dumb, too. I was deaf, dumb, and invisible! Not much different than Lucky.

Nobody worried about what they did or said when Lucky or I was around. I cooked, brought food and drinks into meetings, cleaned up offices and private quarters, and since I was deaf and dumb, everyone's secrets seemed just as safe with me as they were with Lucky. So, last winter, the supervisors took me with them to Connecticut to plan for this year's construction season. I'm what they call a house slave down south. Over the winter I got to stay in the back of a boardinghouse rented by the railroad to house year 'round workers, although I couldn't use the supervisors' privy. But, then, neither could Lucky.

I never did have much to say before the accident, and it seemed best not to say anything afterwards. So I seldom said another word - just did my job and grunted now and then for effect. After awhile it occurred to me that maybe I should just bark when I wanted something – attention, food, or to let someone know something's wrong. Why not? It works for Lucky.

I could tell when the conversation turned to sensitive matters. Men would lean in towards each other, put their heads closer together, and look side to side. If they looked at Lucky, Lucky just ignored them, or he would look up with a dog's grin and his tongue hanging out anticipating a treat. If men in close conversation glanced my direction, I, too, would ignore them, or, just to have fun, I'd give them my doggie smile. Yes, I've learned a lot from that dog.

As my hearing came back I became quite good at not reacting to sound – any sound. While deaf I had become sensitive to vibrations. Doors opening and closing, people walking on floors and stairs, horses in the street, even some deep voices could be felt through the floors and walls. I could tell when someone was walking behind me or walking down a hall or up stairs. By the time my hearing started coming back everyone was convinced I really was deaf. Belknap always explained my presence to others by recounting the premature detonation and joked about how he now had two more mouths to feed: me and Lucky.

Before the great migration I was a teacher in a one-room school-house in Cork, having had the rare privilege of being educated at the Irish College in the Netherlands established by the Church. Most Irish children get no education, but our local priest must have seen something in me, so he tutored me and sent me abroad when I turned thirteen.

After returning to Ireland and during the years leading up to the famine I had a wife, a son, and an acre upon which I grew potatoes. We lived in a windowless mud and straw house with a shed that housed two sheep and a few chickens; an estate by Irish standards. In spite of harassment by the Brits I started a school for the local children and was paid for my teaching with food and handmade clothing by the families of my students.

But the blight started back up in 1840 and got worse each year until there was nothing to harvest and little to eat. The Brits had food, but it was imported and very expensive. As the Famine set in my wife and son fell ill and were lost to consumption. After digging their graves and laying them to rest I had little else to lose, so I decided to seek a better life abroad. Without food a community dies. Cork was dying. Ireland was dying. I wasn't going to die with it.

As far back as anyone can remember my ancestors had owned a good-sized farm in Cork, but with the passing of each generation, the inheritance laws imposed on us by our British occupiers divided each Irish-owned farm into smaller and smaller plots with each passing generation. After only a few generations, the plots were too small to support a family or to farm profitably, and the Brits were there to buy up the bits and pieces. They were then free to re-combine our land and sharecrop our land back to us. The British were buying Ireland at a fire sale – a fire they started and fanned until the whole country was made inhospitable, unless, of course, you were a Lord from London.

Chapter 2

CORDWOOD FOR THE FIRES OF INDUSTRY

This construction season is starting off the same as last. The race to Burlington and beyond to the natural riches of Canada is on. I heard at the company board meetings over the winter that Canadians are building the Vermont & Canada Railroad coming up the Champlain valley, just west over the Green Mountains. We're laying track for the Vermont Central Railroad Company coming up from White River Junction and on through Northfield. We're laying track westerly along the Onion River to Burlington and due north from there.

The Canadians have more miles of rail to lay, but the Champlain valley is flat with few rivers to cross and little elevation change. They even have better weather on the west side of the mountains; an earlier spring and longer fall means longer construction seasons. Our path is shorter, but our route requires moving a lot of earth and rock and building trestles to crisscross a good size river. At the end of last year's season we blasted away the foot of the mountain at the east end of Bolton Flats where Pinneo Brook comes down the west side of the mountain and flows into the Onion. Construction halted in November well short of Pinneo Brook. Blasting made a path wide enough for the rail bed and created rubble for a trestle's footings.

The Vermont Central Railroad's corporate board meets in Connecticut near most of the investors. The bosses on site refer to the Board of Directors as "Fat men running a skinny operation" because the Chairman's annual motivational speech usually contains the phrase "lean and mean." He was right on both counts. The company was lean and

7

mean. Board Chairman, Charles Paine, insists we are losing the race with the V&C. The Vice-chairman of the Board, Mr. Robert Rake, never satisfied except at the dinner table and then not always, uses the phrase "at all costs" to pepper his instructions to Belknap, construction contractor and project manager, and his site bosses Barker, Barnum, Eggleston, and Freeman.

Immigrants have been coming across the ocean all winter to North America stacked like rotting cordwood in the "Coffin Ships." These same ships make the return trip to Europe loaded with the highly prized timber and pelts and other exotic riches from the virgin forests of the New World. For the shipping companies there's an abundance of cargo going each way, but the real moneymaker is the cargo going to England and Europe. We Irish, half dead from starvation, are the backhaul – as long as the ships are returning to pick up more of North America's bounty, might as well take paying passengers.

Our British overlords in Ireland told us we would receive five pounds from a British agent when we landed, but no agents are ever there to greet the new arrivals. Once our poor souls landed in Quebec or Montreal, we were never going to return to Ireland to make a claim. We were promised anything just to get us out of the country – our country, once upon a time.

Two years ago on my ship, the *Jeanne Johnson*, nearly half of the ships' passengers died along the way. Typhus, dysentery, and pneumonia took their toll in the dark, damp, cramped quarters below deck. Those of us who survived the trip to Canada were met on the docks by recruiters for jobs nobody else wanted. Promises of transportation, work, food, and shelter were too good to turn down – no questions asked. Well, none that were answered anyway.

The Company said they needed men to fell timber and clear the road, then lay the bed, lay rail, and build trestles across the rivers. All that desperate labor coming from Ireland and down from Canada was ready-made for the railroads. They offered hope by promising a tent and work and what sounded like a start in the New World. In hindsight we are nothing but fodder feeding the insatiable appetite of unfettered industry.

To a starving man, even a shit sandwich looks good. Having traveled packed into the hull of a ship for two months, crossing the Atlantic during the winter months, seeing more than seventy of your fellow passengers succumb to fever and tossed overboard, and then watching as others were buried stacked on top of one another near the immigration center on Grosse Isle in the middle of the St. Lawrence River – all of that deadens a man's spirits. Hearing any offer of refuge is received like eternal salvation especially after the promise of a British agent meeting us in Montreal is unfulfilled.

Once we were on a buckboard headed to the construction site in the middle of the North Woods, we belonged to the railroad. Before we started work or were even assigned to a tent, we were already in debt. We owed the company fare for the ride to the camps.

.

Chapter 3

INTRODUCTIONS

Looking back, I gotta chuckle. Me pretending to be deaf and dumb and being treated by most as if I were some kind of an intelligent monkey – which, by the way, I think would be a very popular pet if there were such a thing - but the truth is, it took great acting talent and constant concentration for me to be no more than an intelligent monkey. Being deaf following the accident turned out to be a blessing. I did my darnedest to be the best house monkey a house monkey could be.

Belknap is a decent guy. Generally, the bosses don't like to keep the wounded around, but Belknap? Belknap is different. Most people will shoot a crippled dog, but Belknap took one in – two, if you count me. Lucky, who used to be known as Patty, was a hunter, a good bird dog. But a couple of seasons ago, he was left behind or he ran away when the construction season ended. The camp closed up, and Patty was left to fend for himself through a Vermont winter. When management returned to the river valley in the spring to start the next construction season, Lucky was there to greet them, alive, but with a mangled hindquarter likely caused by a wolf, coyote, or a black bear's mauling.

Catherine, that is, Mrs. Dillon, says she found Lucky bleeding and near death under her porch just before Christmas and took him in. Catherine Driscoll Dillon. Now there's an interesting young woman. She and her husband fled Ireland before the famine got too bad. She saw the writing on the wall, came to America, and started selling liquor to workers along the construction route – liquor she smuggles in from Canada.

Her husband, Shamus, is drunk just about every waking moment since coming to America. Childless, Catherine works to support them, and after landing, she saw the potential of turning an empty building into the only boardinghouse within walking distance of a worksite with hundreds of workers and supervisors with money to spend, especially if that boardinghouse serves whiskey.

As the construction crews move on each year, Mrs. Dillon follows them each season as they make their way through the valley to Burlington, relocating her boardinghouse each spring to stay near the workers. Two seasons ago she started adding a tavern to her boardinghouse, and they say her living quarters have gotten nicer each season, too. When the weather ends the construction season, she and her husband find a building or a building site just past where construction ended knowing that's where the next construction season was going to begin. If no existing structure is available, they salvage what they can from the old building and build a new one before the bulk of the season's workers appear.

Last year's roadhouse had their living quarters off the rear of the building and a chicken coop against the back wall. Business must have been good because this year they have their usual tavern, with boarders' rooms above the tavern. But this year their living quarters off the back are two stories tall with glass windows, and the chicken coop is set away from the house next to a shed for their buckboard and two horses.

It's plain to anyone paying attention that Catherine runs their operation, but her husband, Shamus, shouldn't have any complaints because he's become like a barn cat on a dairy farm: ready and eager to lick up any spills, which I have seen him do on more than one occasion. A shame, really. To make matters worse, he's a mean drunk, and he seems to get meaner as his manhood shrivels in relation to his wife's success as a businesswoman.

Catherine nursed Patty, now Lucky, back to health, so this spring Lucky spends his time divided between this season's labor camp being set up on the Flats and enjoying the scraps from the dinner table at Catherine's boardinghouse. The foremen tolerate Lucky because he acts deaf and dumb and stays out of their way - Lesson number one!

Catherine feeds Lucky when he comes around, but apparently he still feels some allegiance to the camp and those who run it. Occasionally,

Catherine disappears for a week at a time, but in her absence her husband, Shamus, doesn't lift a finger for Lucky. At times he can hardly lift a bottle to his own lips.

Supervisor Barnum has arranged a pile of hay in the railroad's tool shed as a bed for Lucky, and sometimes brings him a bone before the cook has a chance to boil the marrow out of it. Lucky spent last winter under Catherine's front porch trying to avoid the boot of her husband. In order to maintain his position in the pecking order, Shamus insults the customers and kicks the dog. So he thinks he's higher in the pecking order than he actually is. Fact is, he isn't even in the pecking order - he doesn't even make a good house monkey.

I guess you'd have to say Catherine is an outlaw, by necessity as she sees it. There are high taxes on the liquor coming in from neighboring states, and the smugglers in any town have enough customers for every bottle they can bring in. So, the only way for Catherine to compete in a man's world, hobbled by her marriage to a drunk, is for her to become a rum-runner, too – bringing it in from nearby Canada. That means she has to cross the border back into the States, not stopping to pay duty or taxes, and to do it without getting caught.

I hear the supervisors say she's gotten caught several times, but she seems to avoid jail by paying a hefty fine, officially or unofficially. Catherine's main obstacle is the local Sheriff, a mean little black Irishman named Ferris. Dark hair, dark skin, and a dark nature, he is a descendent, legend has it, of pre-historic Iberian migrants to the British Isles. Catherine's bane is not the two hundred mile 'round trip to secure Canadian liquor, the brutal weather, the voracious bugs, nor the thieves along the way. No, it's Sheriff Ferris - one mean son of a bitch. Unpleasant by nature, he seems to draw pleasure from his meanness.

Having showed up in Burlington four or five years ago, he said he knew how to handle a pistol and had the deportment of a man in charge of his surroundings. He is particularly proud of the twin double-barreled percussion pistols he keeps tucked in his belt. The North Woods is America's newly settled frontier, and in the absence of civility and established social infrastructure, there's room for an individual to take advantage of the desperate, weak, and fearful, and that's what Sheriff Ferris seems to enjoy doing.

I, too, might have been prey for the sheriff, but Belknap knows my life expectancy outside the camp would be very short after the accident. The explosion had left me with a bad shoulder, so I was no good for physical labor. And, although I was a teacher and journalist in Ireland, being deaf, in a mental fog, and with a bad shoulder in the north woods of America left me little more chance of surviving than any other crippled stray. I was deaf, and, initially, the fog in my head kept me from being able to mumble more than a few disconnected words at a time. It was easier to just gesture for water and grunt than it was to try to ask for it. Belknap gave me water, but, more importantly, he let this crippled stray into management's house.

I survived by becoming management's servant. It took a month for the mental haze to completely lift, and in the meantime, I made myself useful as a butler, errand boy, and cook's assistant. As the fog lifted, my hearing started to come back, but by then I had become more valuable than Lucky. By then I could serve food, fetch cigars and drinks, and provide housekeeping services. The managers had their backwoods version of a gentleman's gentleman, and, best of all, they didn't have to be careful about what they said around me, 'cause I was deaf and dumb - the perfect house monkey!

I can't decide what I'm going to do after the next construction season ends. Lucky and I are getting room and board, but we have little cash. Come next spring, my choice will be to reveal my recovery and resume the life of a desperate Irish laborer, living day-to-day, sleeping in a tent anchored in mud, risking permanent disability or death laying track through the north woods, with no means of support during coming winter, or…..

Or, I could be the best Gentleman's Gentleman I could be 'till we go back down to Connecticut next winter to prepare for the '47 construction season. I'd be living in a boardinghouse and eating good food, even if I must eat in the kitchen. This winter while staying in Connecticut, I was nearly invisible to the kitchen staff, too, since everyone thought I was deaf. I got to hear them talk to each other like I wasn't there. If their masters knew what their own employees were really thinking, they would all sleep with one eye open and a pistol tucked under their pillows if they could sleep at all. One more season as a servant and I'll make my re-entry back into free society. That's my plan.

Chapter 4

THE BOARD

As Belknap's Gentleman, I travel with him to board meetings. Most are in Connecticut, but sometimes the Board comes up to Northfield during construction season. They take the opportunity to hunt and fish under the guise of inspecting the season's worksite, and the stockholders pay for it all. The Board is meeting in Connecticut holding the company's final session before the supervisors head north to start this season. I pour tea as the twelve men around the boardroom table agonize over the financial report in front of them. A tray of biscuits and confections sits untouched in the center of the long mahogany table.

Board Chairman Paine, I'm told, is the son of Elijah Paine, well known for building a turnpike from Brookfield, Vermont, through Northfield, to the Capital, Montpelier, supporting trade between Montreal and Boston. His son, Charles, served as Governor of Vermont a few years back before becoming Chairman of the railroad last year. He delegates the day-to-day responsibilities to Vice-Chairman Rake, a gray-haired ball of fat usually spread out in a chair no part of which is visible. Pompous and dismissive of the help, the Vice Chairman motions me away from the table with a flick of his hand. I become invisible by looking out a window onto the snow-covered streets below.

Paine concludes his remarks, "Those are the numbers, gentlemen. We are over budget and behind schedule. But we can make up for it this season if we have two crews - one laying the bed, while the other builds the trestle."

"Two crews means twice the investment in tools and tents. I don't see how we can afford two crews without additional investors," says Michael Adams, one of the younger board members.

Mr. Rake draws a wheezing breath, "Mr. Adams, we can assess each stockholder an amount to cover the additional expense. If they can't pay the assessment, they'll be forced to surrender their shares and we'll be all the richer. If we don't beat the V & C coming up from Rutland - if we lose this race - the company will be bankrupt, and we can't have that. Call Belknap and Barker to come in."

The young man rose to his feet and opened the door. What I heard from the supervisors was that Michael Adams would not be on the board if Paine didn't need Michael's money, or rather his family's money. Mr. Adams served on several corporate boards, including some local charities, but his father had directed him to be on the railroad board to give him business credentials and a taste of the real world.

Sticking his head into the hall, Michael calls to the two managers, "Mr. Belknap, Mr. Barker, please join us." They enter, hats in hand. "Good day, gentlemen," says Rake, but both men keep their eyes focused on the floor, then glance at each other. Anywhere but into the eyes of Vice Chairman Rake.

"Henry, John, come in," Paine motions them into the room, but not to a seat.

"Belknap," Rake barks, "When can two full crews be in place?"

"Well, um, uh let's see…" Belknap's head turns to look at Barker, then back to Rake, "Well, maybe by the first of the month; certainly by Mid-April," Belknap says with some uncertainty.

Vice Chairman Rake smirks, "Mr. Belknap, the Canadians are laying track half again as fast as we. We're going to have to be…well, creative, or they'll win the race to Rouses Point. Seems the winner will be the company that breaks the most Commandments!" He glances around to see if anyone else shares his sense of humor. No one does. "No excuses, Mr. Belknap. Build the trestle using on-site timbers the way we discussed, and finish five miles of track this season or you'll be out of a job."

Feeling the momentum of his command, Rake turns to the Board and continues, "We're going to improve the way we build trestles, gentlemen."

Gesturing toward the one engineer on the board, "Mr. Stoughton calls it 'pile construction.' Instead of using milled lumber for the verticals, we're going to use half-sawn logs directly from the construction site. And instead of bolting the braces and caps to the posts we're going to use spikes. It'll save us time and money. Mr. Stoughton, will you please describe our new method of construction?"

Mr. Stoughton rises and approaches an easel with a large charcoal drawing of a section of trestle. It was one of the upright verticals in a trestle called a "bent." A bent looks like the letter "A" but with the top cut off and one or two additional verticals and cross pieces. He's confident rough timber can replace the more expensive milled timbers for the vertical structure of each bent, and instead of bolting the cross braces to the verticals, we will use large spikes, again saving time because we won't have to drill holes, and we will also save the expense of using much more expensive nuts and bolts. He seems very pleased with himself, and gets an approving nod from Mr. Rake when his presentation is done.

Michael's gaze into Rake's eyes intensifies, "Where has this been done before, Robert? I'd like to inspect an example of this method you're recommending."

"I don't believe it has been done before, Mr. Adams," Rake proudly replies. "That's one of the beauties of business - competition spurs innovation. We'll win this race with innovation!" Rake's fist hits the table for emphasis.

"But it's not beautiful when innovation fails, Mr. Rake. I don't have your confidence in the integrity of a structure that's not bolted. It just doesn't seem right to experiment..."

Rake interrupts Michael, "Right? The only morality in business, Mr. Adams, is to play by the rules, and there are no rules about how we build a trestle. This isn't church, Mr. Adams. Competition in industry rewards innovation, not morality. As long as the rules of the game allow a short-cut, then a businessman, in order to stay in business, is compelled to take the short cut." Rake smiles as he looks at each board member digest his impeccable logic.

Michael bristles, "This is not a game, Sir. Your 'innovation' may be risking men's lives. You could incite the second Bolton Massacre!"

Michael is referring to the storming of the parliamentarian town of Bolton, England, by the Royalists during the English civil war two centuries earlier. The informal conventions of honorable warfare were cast aside when the Royalists, in support of the monarchy, attacked the town at night without the usual courtesy of offering surrender, or at least negotiation. Because the attack took place on the city streets, at night and without warning, it was difficult to distinguish soldier from civilian, so both were massacred.

"I have no objection to competing with the same restrictions as my rivals," says Paine entering the fray. "It's the government's responsibility to write the rules of the game, and our duty is to play by those rules while insuring a profit for our shareholders."

Rake breaks in, "The rules of trestle construction allow this method of construction, and if it gives us an advantage over our competition, Sir, then, we are compelled to do it."

Silence hangs in the air. Rake's reasoning seems to have overpowered caution and compassion. Chairman Paine turns toward Michael, "Mr. Adams, this is our own innovation. Mr. Stoughton assures me such construction will be adequate until we replace the trestle with iron as planned. We'll continue to use milled timber for the stringers on top so the ties will rest securely on a flat surface."

Mr. Stoughton's failure to defend the design prompts Michael to turn to him, "You have confidence in this method, Mr. Stoughton?"

Rake knows what's coming and is ready to interrupt. Mr. Stoughton acknowledged that spikes wouldn't be as secure as bolts, but when cross-examined by Paine he did acknowledge that wood trestles are meant to be temporary structures, and the plan is to replace the Bolton trestle with iron before it got much use.

Stoughton returns to his easel and goes on to describe another major difference with the new design: instead of the vertical posts being tied together with a sill at the bottom, each post will be hewn to a point, and a horizontal cross-piece will be spiked into the posts several feet up from the bottom; the idea being the sharpened posts will sink into the river bed and hold the bent in place and then rip-rap will be dropped around the posts for added stability.

Paine concludes the discussion about the trestle this way, "Until there's a law that says we can't build it using our new method, we're going to do it. We're in a race to the border, and having competition means we have to take advantage of every short cut as we are able."

Paine turns to Mr. Belknap for his update. Belknap reports, "We have timber for the trestle being cut now, before the sap rises, and Barnum and Eggleston are in Montreal recruiting more labor. We will have more than one hundred men there in late March ready to work. Fifty are there now setting up the storage shed, tents, and the store. We'll cut timber while the ground's still frozen and stack it by the trench saw."

"I want more men working this year - two hundred," says Chairman Paine.

"Then we'll need at least half again as many buckboards and drivers and more supplies," says Mr. Belknap.

Rake seems irritated, "You won't need the buckboards if you make additional trips. Find a few trustworthy men among the first group in camp and send them back to the port for the rest of the labor needed. As for the additional supplies, we'll take care of that. You just worry about getting the men in place. Can you do that? Can you do that, Mr. Belknap?"

"Yes, sir, but I...."

"Yes?" snaps Rake.

"We'll be buying supplies at the last minute. It'll be expensive, and we'll need more tents and provisions right away."

Rake's face is bright red. "You're going to have to make do with the number of tents ordered and on hand for now. We'll see what we can do about getting more. In the meantime we've ordered more provisions - enough for the season to get started. As for cash, there's already a month's payroll in the bank in Northfield, and we'll send up more when we get it."

"He'll need it right away," Mr. Adams interjects. Rake's eyes blaze at Adams as he struggles to turn in his chair. Michael continues, "Transporting the workers from Montreal and setting up the camp will take half of it, and we already have a payroll to meet for the men cutting timber."

"God damn it, he'll get it when he needs it, Mr. Adams. Have you got any questions, Belknap?"

"Well, sir…"

Rake interrupts, "And what about Mrs. Dillon? Is she still there?"

"Yes, sir. But…"

"Damn it, man, I thought we got rid of her last year," says Rake.

"She's bought a cabin on the Stage Road toward Jonesville and hired away four of our men to add on to it," reports Mr. Belknap.

Michael stands up and faces Rake, "What do you mean 'we got rid of her last year'?"

"Relax, Mr. Adams. Seems her husband was drunk and knocked over a lamp. There was a fire. Such accidents do happen. I simply meant I did not expect her to be able to re-build, that's all. Anything else, Belknap?"

"No, sir." Belknap, not waiting to be formally dismissed, backs toward the door and exits quickly. I turn from the window as the door closes behind Belknap.

"Mr. Paine," Michael's voice is stern as he comes around the table and walks toward him. "Mr. Paine, I will not be a party to criminal behavior."

"Michael," Rake looks up at the young man, "We have a railroad to build. I don't care about Mrs. Dillon. Let her have her fucking tavern. We'll keep the men too busy to drink." Paine and others laugh.

Rake continues, "I move we adopt the proposed budget presented by Mr. Mazer and assess each shareholder ten dollars a share to be paid by April first. Those who can't pay will have to surrender their shares, and we will have the right of first refusal to purchase them. All in favor? "

Not waiting for a second to the motion, each says "Aye" in turn. "It's settled, then. I'll have Mr. Walton notify the shareholders. I expect each of you to have your assessments here by close of business this Friday coming. We need to get additional supplies and workers to the site and get them to work as quickly as possible. Is there any other business? No? Then we should be well under way by the time we meet again in April. I move we adjourn. All in favor?"

"Aye," is said in unison.

"Good day, gentlemen," says Paine.

"Good day, Mr. Paine. Gentlemen," says Michael looking at each man; some returning knowing glances, others not meeting his gaze. He gathers his papers, places them in his briefcase, and walks to the door. Michael stops, looks back, and draws a breath as if to speak. Instead, he turns and walks out.

I begin to remove the refreshments and wipe down the conference table. Rake closes the door and looks at Treasurer Mazer. "Simon, is that black Irishman, Sheriff Ferris, still in Richmond?"

"Why, yes, I believe he is."

Rake takes an envelope from his breast pocket and stuffs it into Mazer's hand, "Good. Give this to Belknap for Sheriff Ferris. We can't afford any more problems this year. We'll have the men, and soon we'll have the money. We should reach the lake by '49 – maybe as much as a year ahead of the Rutland gang. God willing, nothing is going to stop us!"

Chapter 5

WE DIDN'T TAKE THE SOUP

I arrived in North America two years ago, and shortly after I landed for the following year I was a laborer for the railroad. Last season I became a Gentleman's Gentleman, and now we're headed back up north to start another construction season. I tell ya, everywhere ya go you can feel the momentum building in the States fueled with money and a burgeoning population. Money and poor mongrels desperate to simply eat are feeding industry. Fortunes are being made and lost and made again by those who are first, lucky, or well connected.

The corporate boardrooms are where plots are hatched against the competition and some against nature herself. Mountains are moved and rivers crossed; people are consumed like coal feeding a boiler, and the railroads of New England had a taste for the Irish. We were pushed into the sea by famine, and merchant ships brought whole villages across the ocean to the New World. Landing in Quebec City and Montreal, we arrived with no more than we could carry and were easy prey for the labor contractors who promised food, shelter, and jobs. What choice did we have? Stay home and die of starvation, or give yourself up to whatever fates await in a land unknown.

We did have one other option. The Brits occupying Ireland had enough food to feed us all, and they did set up soup kitchens. So, we had the option of taking the soup. But, before we could take the soup we had to renounce the Catholic faith and convert to the Brits' Protestant religion. Some choice! Take the soup, live another day, and burn in hell for eternity, or starve to death and hope your faith in the Pope and the

Catholic church gets us into Heaven until the end of time. Needless to say, those of us who fled our homeland didn't take the soup. The question that remains is: what is it we will be asked to endure if we take the railroad's soup?

It's late March, and winter in Vermont is not yet over. Another ship packed with refugees arriving as sure as the tides has entered the mouth of the Saint Lawrence ready to disgorge its human cargo. Word on the dock is that more than thirty ships with as many as three thousand immigrants aboard are anchored in the river, waiting out their fifteen days in quarantine on Grosse Isle, just downstream of Quebec. The lice-infested holds of the ships spread Typhus among the passengers and take as many lives as the starvation they left behind.

When the planks hit the dock in Montreal, I see men, women, and children dragging satchels and sacks standing anxiously on deck waiting to take their first steps into their futures. "Good-byes" had been said, and the passengers who had survived the voyage gathered their belongings and jostled for position near the gangplanks. Once on the dock the new arrivals look in futility for the British agents they were told would meet them, but no agents are to be found. Instead, they're told to move along, and move along, they do; right into the waiting arms of my employer!

Chapter 6

ONE MORE MURPHY

Maurice Murphy stands tall on deck; his teenage daughter's hand in his. "Is this where we are going to live?" asks Christine.

"We're getting off here. We'll live where I can find work, Sweetheart. We're in Canada, and just south of here is the United States of America. The ship's crew told me there's plenty of work for anyone who wants to work."

As the crew throw lines to the waiting hands on the dock, others move the gangplank into position. People start moving, picking up bundles, trunks, and children. When the ship is secure and the gangplank in place, the first passengers climb three steps to the rail and start down the plank to their new lives. A swarm of bedraggled men and women are on the move, flowing onto the dock and flooding the town with renewed hope.

Men, women, children, horses, buckboards, and cargo are all moving this way and that on the dock. Voices can be heard above the din calling for family members to stay together. People are being pushed and pulled; separated and reunited. Men off-loading cargo are shouting orders and directing the laborers.

Other voices like barkers at a carnival are heard above the crowd. "Honest work in the United States! Free land! Free passage to the States, sign up here!" Half a dozen men are standing on crates and the back of buckboards shouting to the crowd, "Honest work for honest men. Food, shelter, and passage to the States!"

"Hey!" Maury shouts back to one of the recruiters getting his attention, "Hey! Pardon me, Sir. I'm looking for a Mr. Spector. He's a Hudson Bay Company agent. He is….." The recruiter cut him off mid-sentence.

"I don't know a Mr. Spector, and I don't know what you were told, but you're not going to find any agent from the Hudson Bay Company here to meet you. But, I can offer you work in the states and the start you're looking for. What's your name, and how many in your party?"

Maury looks at his daughter, then asks, "What's the work?"

"Sign up here and I'll provide you and your family shelter, food, and passage to New England. How many men in your family?"

"What's the work?"

"We're laying railroad track through some of the most beautiful land on God's green earth. We'll pay each man fifty cents a day, six and a half days a week for thirty weeks. That's nearly one hundred American dollars! You could start a whole new life with a hundred dollars couldn't you? What's your name?"

"Murphy, but I'm not interested."

"You won't find a better offer. Too many like you looking for something better, but it ain't here." The barker turns back to the crowd, "Honest work in the Colonies! Free land! Free passage to the States." Others approach the man.

"Let's find Joseph." Maury says to his daughter. He approaches the window of a ticket agent, "Pardon me, sir, I'm looking for a blacksmith named McCarthy."

"All the blacksmiths are on Rue Sainte Catherine - that way," he says pointing over his shoulder, "But McCarthy closed up shop one day last month and hasn't been seen since."

Away from the docks the streets are less crowded. Each street is a half frozen mixture of mud and horse manure. The bundled pair first come across two saloons separated by a general store. They slog their way across the street and up onto a wooden walk in front of a store with a glass window behind which is a saddle on display. "Stay right here while I see if they know of Joseph's whereabouts," and Maury disappears inside.

Less than a minute later he reappears and puts his arm around his daughter's shoulders, "The man says McCarthy died several weeks ago. 'Says it was consumption, maybe Pneumonia. He doesn't know where his help went."

Maury and Christine return to the docks where he approaches the recruiter, and not having an alternative, agrees to join the man's crew.

Chapter 7

THE ROAD TO SALVATION

Misery has been a constant for the last two or three years for everyone touched by the famine. The black, slimy, potato rot set in hard in '44, destroying the primary crop most Irish farms produced. As the previous years' edible stores were consumed, death came first to the poor, while others hung on thinking the next harvest would bring relief. But there was no relieve. The blight spread, and as their misery grew people were forced to flee their homes and abandon their livelihoods leaving the dead and dying behind. Death and disease chased men, women, and children onto boats and into the frigid North Atlantic as the winter of 1845-46 took hold.

An air of doom and desperation clung to the emotionally weary and physically weakened refugees. Clothing didn't get washed more than once during the journey, and only then in a bath of salt water. The ship owners are required to provide one pound of food per passenger per day, but stores were usually short because voyages would be calculated to take twenty-eight days, when most took anywhere from forty to ninety days, and then there was the assumption that the passenger count would "shrink" during the voyage. Those calculations caused food shortages on most crossings. Even so, although most new arrivals start the voyage emaciated from the famine, many look well fed as they disembark because they wear most of the clothing they own to keep out the chill of the North Atlantic and the Canadian winter.

Tonight, though, is different. Having accepted the offers of the recruiters tonight is the first night in a thousand when an air of hope is shared by the new arrivals unaffected by the broken promises of the agents and uncertain futures. There is warmth and hope coming simply from being together, alive, and standing on land in a new world.

All of the recruiters hand out biscuits to their new hires. A few offer a night's stay in a hotel if the poor critters agree to sign up. Our terms of employment are always better than the others. The only difference is that our competitors usually have every good intention of honoring their agreement. Contrary to our recruiters' description of our itinerary, we are going directly to the season's worksite from the dock without the benefit of a night in a hotel. If the trip to the camps is slowed by weather or road conditions, we may stop and let them sleep in a barn; but there'd be no better overnight refuge for our refugees.

But what's a man to do? Alone or with family, it's winter in Canada; there's no agent to meet the new arrivals; and no apparent alternative but to succumb to a recruiter's siren song. Just as they were carried by the currents of the sea to North America, they were swept up in the flow of humanity leaving the ships and into the unknown in a strange land.

I watch as recruits sign up one man after another. All who agree are loaded onto the waiting buckboards to begin the twenty-hour trip to the construction site 'bout five miles east of Jonesville, Vermont. We load them eighteen at a time onto four buckboards to be transported from their deepening desperation to the budding dawn of hope. Tonight is bitter cold and a biting north wind is at our backs, pushing us south into the states. Strangers and clan members huddle together under blankets provided by the company. Children are held close and sleep.

I sit next to Barnum driving the lead wagon south out of Montreal; first through village streets, then out into fields and through woodlands with a light snow falling. There are few boardinghouses between Montreal and Highgate, the first settlement in the United States. We continue on through Burlington, a well-established town on the shore of Lake Champlain, without stopping. Barnum, thinking he's talking only to himself, repeatedly curses the cold.

With Burlington ten miles behind, we stop at a small farm, and all are told to take our blankets into the hayloft for what remained of the night. The supervisors stay in the farmhouse, but I have to make do staying with the recruits. At first I'm peppered with questions, but I just point to my ears, shake my head, and bark, "Derf!" startling small children. Even if I choose to answer, some questions I can't answer in full honesty, so I don't answer any. Most often asked: Are the roads really paved with gold? That's an easy one: No. Finding a job with the railroad is a blessing? The honest answer: not likely.

Next morning we load up for the push to the construction site on Bolton Flats. A few minutes east of Richmond, we pass a stagecoach heading west to Burlington, and the children strain to get a look at the six prancing horses, two by two, their noses snorting steam and straining against their harnesses, pulling the enclosed wooden coach.

We pass through Jonesville, five miles west of the Flats where the camps are being set up for the season. The company supervisors usually stay in the hotel in Jonesville where there is a general store that also serves as the post office. The hitching posts in front of the general store have a couple of saddled horses tied up, and they glance at us as we pass, then casually turn back to staring at the ground.

Across from the hotel is a large building belching heavy smoke from a brick chimney running up its center. The ping of a blacksmith's hammer comes from the open doors. We push on without stopping.

Chapter 8

DUBLIN AND CORK

The month of March in Vermont, in fact anywhere north of Massachusetts, is cold and damp and windy, with snow still deep in the northern valleys. The daytime sun is starting to get high enough in the sky to melt the frozen earth exposed on the Stage Road, turning it to sticky mud during the day, and then freezing rutty and hard as rock overnight. Today is cold and likely to stay cold, so the still frozen road tests the strength of the buckboards and tosses our passengers about like drops of water dancing on a hot skillet. Choose your poison: neck-breaking jolts bumping across frozen ruts, or dodging dollops of mud thrown up in the air by hoof and wheel.

Barnum is driving our horses, and I'm next to him; both of us bundled up so we look like one big pile of blankets with the reins disappearing into a fold. As the buckboards are tossed from side to side the harnesses rattle and the leaf springs squeak. Another two hours pass mostly in silence. The children are used to the movement of the buckboards, reminiscent of the motion of the ship they just left, so they nap. The grownups are straining to see around the next bend, quietly chatting, or giving into their fatigue, heads bowed, wrapped in wool against the cold.

As the wagons draw to a halt, Barnum, in the lead wagon, stands up and turns around to address the crowd, "Stay in the wagons until I am through with my instructions." Several of our site supervisors with long guns are here to meet the arrivals, along with the General Contractor and Site Manager Belknap holding the company's ledger.

Barnum continues, "One family or worker at a time may get down from the wagon, with your possessions, give your name to Mr. Belknap, and follow these men across the footbridge to your tent site. Any items left in the wagons will become the properly of the railroad. Food has been prepared, and you can pick up one day's provisions at the camp store after supper," he says, pointing to a log cabin across the river in the center of the Flats with two lit lanterns one hanging on each side of the front door.

"From now on, each family will be responsible for providing for themselves or purchasing whatever you need at the camp store. Each man will have an account at the camp store. What you spend at the store will be deducted from your pay. Your pay will be three dollars and twenty-five cents a week, and we work half days Sunday, rain or shine. Any questions?" Silence. As names are called, passengers disembark from the wagons, cross the footbridge, and are guided by others to tents already set up in the snow-covered field.

Cold and hungry, I head directly to the warmth of Mrs. Dillon's boardinghouse – seeking the sources of warmth I know I'll find there. Barnum had given me most of my meager wages for March when we arrived at the camps weeks earlier, and I want to spend a little bit of it: warm up by the Franklin stove, sip some tolerable whiskey, and spend time with Catherine and Lucky. I will have plenty of work to do soon enough.

Last summer the rail bed had ended well before a bend in the river caused by an escarpment jutting out from the foot of the mountains on the north side of the river and forcing the river to make a bend around the rock. The railroad needs to cross from the north side of the river to the south side in order to continue its run west. So a trestle over the river will have to be built, and our engineer's new design will have that trestle constructed with timbers cut from the surrounding woods instead of the milled and dried timber from the sawmills in Waterbury, Middlesex, and Barre.

Over the centuries the river had cut a deep path through the mountains, heading west to Lake Champlain. The trestle will need to be anchored to each shore by an approach, a stone structure made by laying several layers of stone into the bank where the structure will begin its course over the river. From what I understand each vertical segment of the trestle will be constructed on shore, slid into the water upstream of its intended resting place, and floated into position. All the pieces will be tied together to form a bridge strong enough to carry a locomotive and a few heavily loaded cars to support the laying of track to Burlington and eventually up to the Canadian border. The wooden trestle will be replaced by an iron bridge once a train can bring the tons of necessary material.

The Stage Road follows the river from Montpelier to Burlington. The rail line comes up from Northfield, and meets the river just west of Montpelier. One bounty of the North Woods is the granite found in the quarries of Northfield and Barre. Granite's in great demand in Boston and Hartford to construct buildings to house the living and for markers to commemorate the dead. The railroad had come up to Northfield and Barre years earlier, and ended there until a spur continued north another seven miles to Montpelier, the state's capitol. Nowadays, the Stage Road is the only means of conveyance east and west through central Vermont's Green Mountains running north and south.

Supervisors Barker and Eggleston are making their usual rounds giving each tent the same speech, "After tonight, you'll be responsible for feeding yourselves. There's a general store in Jonesville, and a wagon makes one round trip each day – first six onboard can go - no charge. If you're not going to cook for yourself, before sundown you'll hear a gun shot followed by a bell ringing. That will be the signal to bring the largest pot in your gear to the store to pick up your dinner. Each quart will be ten cents. If you need a pot or cooking gear you can come to the store and purchase it on account against your earnings."

They conclude saying, "Tomorrow, a supervisor will come around just after dawn to tell you more and answer your questions. All men fifteen years and older should be ready to work."

With that, Barker and Eggleston turn and disappear into the sea of tents, wandering through the two camps for the entire evening giving the same speech and answering as few questions as possible.

Chapter 9

SETTING DOWN STAKES

The railroad provided the essentials to establish the encampments. Most of the new recruits have some provisions with them, a trunk or a bag or two of personal possessions, while a few others have only the clothes on their backs. But for all, this is the foothold they need to feel they have made their escape from the persistent oppression of the British and the black rot that caused the famine.

Although fresh water is available from the main river, the water is sweeter from Pinneo Brook, a small stream coming down from the mountains and running along the east border of the Flats. A log has been felled just above where the Pinneo flows into the Onion, the main River, and that log is in almost constant use as a privy as are the two outhouses near the center of the Flats' north tree line.

In the fading light the whole of incoming workers and their families divide into smaller communities by re-pitching their tents closer together, and divide again into groups by placing five or six tents so they face one another to share a campfire built on the frozen mud. The company had set the tents up in rows, each of two rows facing one another. But there seems to be an inherent drive in we humans to establish communities and to nurture a sense of belonging. Without discussion new arrivals realign tents into wilderness communities and then into the equivalent of neighborhoods amplifying their sense of a shared experience.

A woman under a tattered scarf stops by the Murphy's tent. "You might want the children to go gather some firewood before it gets too dark. Otherwise, they'll charge you a bit for an armload from the railroad's stockpile."

Maury looks up, "The railroad's stockpile?"

"The railroad's store of firewood. They have us cut it down during the day, then sell it back to us at night. They'd charge you for taking a breath if they could," she says.

"Thank you for the advice. How long have you been here?"

"We got to Montreal a week ago, and have been here five days. We already owe the boss two bits for wood and five cents for two spoons. Be careful what you ask for." She fades back into the twilight as quickly as she had appeared.

The newly arrived families tend to speak in whispers that grow louder as tents are erected and fires lit. The children sense they are starting to become part of a community, and their voices laced with laughter can be heard above others. The campfires and the sparks they release into the sky push back the descending darkness; adding to the accumulating light and warmth of the evening. So many fires have been lit that they illuminate a golden cloud of wood smoke hanging over the valley.

As the darkening night gives way to the glow of warming fires, voices become lighter and laughter punctuates the din. There's a comfort taking hold along with a sense of relief. Back home, the famine had the upper hand. It forced families from their homes; it took pride, dignity, hope, and, finally, a sense of belonging from all in her grip. It tore communities asunder, ripping families apart, and sending all who were able into the foreboding Atlantic in search of survival. Bolton Flats had become a castaway's refuge; a welcome foothold in the New World.

A man and his wife had just finished pitching their tent on the opposite side of the fire in front of the Murphy's tent. "Hello, neighbor!" says the husky man, his hand extended. "The name is Patrick, Patrick O'Reilly."

Maury, responds, glad to hear a hearty welcome, "Hello! My name is Maurice. Maurice Murphy," and pointing to the undulating walls of his tent, "And in there is my daughter, Christine."

"Glad to meet you, Maury. Where're you from?"

"From just outside of Kilkenny - Greystroke. We sailed from Kilrane. And you?"

"We're from Cork…" But before Patrick could finish his thought, bang! A rifle shot tore through the night, and bang, bang, bang echoed across the valley. The single shot, by itself wouldn't normally startle anyone, but multiplied by the steep mountains, it was heard by some as an unexpected onslaught. Many of the newcomers instinctively duck thinking there is a volley being exchanged. But, a ringing bell brings everyone's attention back to the matters at hand, and the new recruits start to walk toward the company store eager to retrieve a hot meal.

"Come on, Maury. Let's see what's going on."

"Can I go, Father?" Christine asks.

"No, you stay here, Sweetheart. Be ready to eat when we get back."

"But I want to come and see!"

"Children are supposed to do what they're told!" He says as he lays his hand on Christine's head and rumbles her hair.

"I'm fourteen!" protests Christine, "I'm hardly a child."

Maury and Patrick join a flowing stream of men and women making their way to the camp store.

Chapter 10

FIRST NIGHT

After I helped prepare the evening meal of oatmeal, dried cod, and biscuits, and before the dinner bell is rung, I walk in the light drizzle through the maze of tents frequently pointing to my ears, shaking my head, and smiling whenever someone tries to talk to me. I hear someone say, "Poor critter is deaf and dumb. I think he works for the railroad."

Hey! Don't we all? I'm not just some homeless mongrel hoping to be tossed a scrap of bread, which reminds me: I haven't seen Lucky lately.

Two of the supervisors who joined us last year, Jonathan Eggleston and Benjamin Freeman, stand together on the store's front porch. Eggleston addresses the waiting crowd, "Anyone needing a cooking pot or other utensils should go around to the back of the store. You'll need it if you're going to eat from the company pot.

A few people leave the line and head to the rear of the store passing others making their way back to the front. "How long will it take us to pay for this pot?" one man asks holding it up for Eggleston, busy recording the names of those in line, to see.

The man walking behind him answers, "Two bits. I was told they're paying us fifty cents a day, so you already owe them half a day."

"You owe them more than that," says another voice from the rear. "The ride here cost you a half dollar each, and if you slept in a barn on your trip here it cost you another dime a head."

Maury and Patrick are in line and approach the platform. On the porch Eggleston is seated at a table with a ledger. Without looking up he says, "Name?"

"O'Reilly. Patrick O'Reilly."

"Middle name?"

"David."

"Wife's name?"

"My wife's name? Why do you need to know that?"

"So far we have two Patrick David O'Reilly's here, and we need next of kin. Wife's name?"

"Kathleen. Next of kin? My wife's my next of kin."

"What is your profession?"

"I'm an engineer. A civil engineer."

The man at the table takes interest. Lifting his head to look at Patrick, "Yeah? What have you built?"

"Roads and bridges, mostly."

The man makes a note, "Ten cents."

"Ten cents? For what?"

"For the hot meal you are about to get. Do you have a pot?"

"Yeah, I have one, but I'll have to go back and get it," says Patrick.

"Don't bother." Reaching down to a stack of metal bowels nested in a stack, "Bring this back later tonight - washed." The man makes another mark next to Patrick's name and hands him a battered metal pail from the stack. "Return it before you go to sleep."

"Next. Name?"

"Murphy.....Maurice Robert Murphy."

"Occupation?"

"Carpenter and cabinetmaker."

"That'll be ten cents."

Maury reaches into his pocket and takes out several coins, holding his hand open. "How much is that in Shillings?"

The man picks a coin out of Maury's outstretched hand, "Next." The coin went into a metal box.

Steam rises from a large pot on the table. Another covered pot is sitting on the porch. Patrick puts his bowl on the table, and a man dips a large metal cup into the steam coming up from the chunky oatmeal stew and dumps its contents into Patrick's pot. Patrick can see a few chunks of potato, carrots, and onions in the oatmeal. It smells good. "Is that all?" he asks.

"Another dip will be another ten cents," comes the answer.

"This'll do. Thank you," says Patrick. The next man behind the table hands Patrick a small bundle wrapped in brown paper. He unwraps it and looks inside. The aroma coming off of two fresh-baked biscuits warms his nose. "Christ, Maury! Smell that!" He waves the biscuits under Maury's nose.

"Let's get back to the girls," says Maury, pointing the way to their tent site.

Both families stand around the fire, Maury and Christine passing the pot back and forth. Small talk continues between mouthfuls of warm stew and biscuits.

As night closes in most of the fires fade to coals. Maury and Patrick take turns going to the edge of the woods, breaking dead branches from the trees to keep their fire burning.

During one trip to the woods to retrieve firewood, Maury encounters another man doing the same. "G'd evening," says Maury in a low voice."

"Aye, to you, too, sir," comes the reply. "Where ya from?"

"'Just outside of Kilkenny," says Maury, "and you?"

"From Dublin," replies the man. "In fact, we call our camp on the west side of the Flats 'Dublin,' so I guess I'm still from Dublin."

An island of rocks and trees divides the otherwise open flat in half. The company's store is placed between it and the road. The man points to the collection of tents on the other side of the divide.

"We've been here almost a week, and the woods on our side are pretty well picked clean. But some of us do keep our fires going overnight so everyone will have some heat in the morning. No one is going to take care of us unless we take care of ourselves." The man pauses and looks like he's about ready to say something else, but doesn't.

After a moment he continues, "There are maybe a hundred families on our side, and the boss says you'll have a hundred on yours by the end of the week."

"Two hundred families?" Maury says, astonished.

"About three hundred good souls on our side now, counting the women and children. They say the company ran a construction camp like this last year, and they seem to know what they're doing. Life is still hard, but at least there's food and shelter."

"I'm Maury Murphy," Maury says holding out his hand, " and I'm here with my daughter, Christine."

"Pleasure. I'm Thomas….Noonan. My wife's name is Abigail. We have four children with us and left two behind, God rest their souls." He makes the sign of the Cross across his chest.

Maury looks at him and now sees more than just another man carrying wood. Once you begin to know a person's story his appearance changes. "I'm sorry. I lost my wife to consumption, and when I laid our youngest, my boy Ian, to rest I knew it was time to do something drastic, so here we are."

The two stood silently, each remembering the parts of themselves they had left behind buried Ireland's good earth.

"Will you be cutting timber tomorrow?" asks Thomas.

"All I know is a foreman will come around first thing in the morning to answer our questions."

"My guess is you wouldn't be here if you had much money, so you'd better gather your own wood until the real work begins. Besides, it'll keep you warm and warm you twice: when you collect it and when you burn it. And you be sure to ask a boss about pay," Thomas says with a smile. "Haven't gotten a straight answer on that one yet. Perhaps I'll see you again. Take care."

"Good night to you, too, Mr. Noonan." And the men return to gathering an armful of wood.

That night, Maury and Christine sleep side by side under several blankets and still in the clothes they wore on the crossing.

Chapter 11

DAWN DAY ONE

Maury awoke when the first light of day pierced the crisp cold air making his breath visible. Christine remained asleep as he carefully rolled out from under the blanket and backed out of the tent. Outside, a light snow is falling on Patrick as he stares at the fire with a flask in his hand; and his hand inside a sock for warmth. The fire is aflame and warm with a healthy pile of wood nearby.

In a whisper Patrick says, "Good morning, Maury."

" 'Morning, Patrick. The fire looks good - feels good, too. You get any more sleep?"

"A little more," and seeing Maury looking at his bottle, in a hushed voice Patrick says, "Thought I'd warm myself up with a little fortification before breakfast." He pushes the cork back into the flask and puts it back inside his coat pocket.

Just as Maury is about to say something, a voice breaks the dawn's cold stillness. "Gentlemen! Over here and listen up."

Maury takes a few steps toward the man. It's Barker. With a hushed voice Maury asks, "Could you keep your voice down, please? My daughter's very tired after the journey and she needs her rest."

"This is a work camp," Barker says as he turns toward the store. Within a few minutes most of the men in the camp had gathered in front of the store and Barker addresses them from the porch. "My name is Barker. I'm a supervisor here along with several others," he points to each of the men standing behind him, "Namely Mr. Barnum, Mr. Eggleston, and Mr. Freeman. You and I work for Mr. Belknap and the

Vermont Central Railroad Company. We will be laying about five miles of track this season starting from just around the bend," he says pointing east, "and continuing to the other side of the river and west to Jonesville, 'bout five miles west."

Several men back away to keep from being hit as Barker's arm traced the planned path of the track with a motion like a scythe through tall grass.

"The tracks we laid last year end a hundred yards past the Brook at the east end of the Flats," he says pointing east.

He then turns back around and points across the river to the frozen bank on the other side. "We'll have a crew building a trestle to cross the river, and another crew preparing the rail bed and laying track."

The main river makes a wide turn to the south in order to get around the foot of the mountains. It dug a sharp bank at least twelve feet high where it flowed against the rock on the far side and was forced back toward the west, cutting an "S" and a narrow pass through the spine of mountains running north and south, from Canada to Massachusetts. Chunks of ice are stacked in a jumble on the far side just up stream of the spot where Barker says the trestle is to go.

Barker continues, "Anyone with logging or construction experience see me at the store just after you see the sun come up. Likely you'll be on crew number one, assigned to the trestle. The rest of you will be working on preparing the bed, cutting timber, or laying track. Are there any questions?"

Mr. Barker hesitates, but before anyone could get a question out, he turns, and the sea of men part to let him through.

Maury and Patrick get in a line snaking between the tents closest to the store. Hanging over a fire is a boiling pot, each bubble belching a puff of steam into the cold morning air. As they approach, they can see it's another dose of oatmeal. Each man in line is served from the pot, giving his name to Supervisor Barnum before returning to his tent.

The sky is deep blue for an hour before the sun rises from behind the eastern horizon. Living in the shadow of the mountains prolongs the cold in the morning air. The muddy field has frozen overnight, and boots left outside a tent are frozen to the ground and dusted with a light cover of snow.

Later, men gather again at the store where two tables are set up, one at each end of the front porch. A man comes out of the store with a blanket held up in the air with one hand and a knife held high in the other. He stabs the blanket, the point of the knife catching the cloth, and he cuts a twelve inch slit in the blanket's center. Putting his knife back in its sheathe, the man removes his hat, sticks his head through the hole in the blanket, and puts his hat back on. Reaching into a pouch on his belt, he removes a small rope and ties it around his waist so that the blanket appears to become a monk's frock. Standing in front of the store and having the attention of most there, he's compelled to speak.

"The good Lord didn't save us from the famine to be fodder for a railroad. We prayed for deliverance once, and our prayers were answered. Maybe we should be prayin' again."

He looks at the surprised faces looking back at him and the annoyed expressions on the supervisors' faces. He steps down and melts into the crowd.

Patrick turns to Maury, "What was that about?"

"I guess some men are never satisfied, says Maury. "We'd better find out what happens next."

A young man comes out of the store and onto the front porch and addresses the growing crowd. "My name is Eggleston, Jonathan Eggleston. Mr. Barnum and I will be in charge of the trestle crew. Any men who have construction experience should form a line at this table. All others see Mr. Barker at the other table," he says pointing to the far end of the platform where Barker is coming to his feet.

Barker has a big smile on his face, "Mr. Eggleston is a junior engineer from Boston. The heaviest tool he ever lifts is a pencil! We'll be doin' the real work of building a railroad. The rest of you, let me have your attention."

About half the men drift toward Mr. Barker's table. Maury turns to go toward the trestle crew when Patrick grabs his arm. "Maury, you don't want to work on the trestle. It sounds dangerous. Can you swim?" Maury shook his head. Patrick continues, "Building a trestle..... I don't know. Think you might rather stay on the ground.

"They need men who have experience road-building, so maybe you'd better go over there, says Maury pointing to Barker. "I helped the town build a bridge and kinda enjoyed it. Got real satisfaction every time I went over it. I'm signing up for the trestle crew." Maury heads toward Mr. Eggleston's table.

Patrick hesitates, watching Maury's back. "Damn!" he says under his breath, and takes a few quick steps to catch up to Maury, but then stops, and turns back toward Barker's table. Again reversing his course and joining his friend, "I hope I don't regret this, Mr. Murphy."

Maury turns toward Patrick, "I bet you have the experience they're lookin' for."

"Never built a trestle, but I figure I can learn," says Patrick.

Patrick and Maury join the rear of the cluster of men at trestle sign-up. Before they reach the table, Mr. Eggleston stands up and says, "That's all. We got all we need for the trestle, but we still need ten sawyers and twenty to hew and notch logs." When the sign-up was all over, Maury and Patrick had joined the logging crews.

They return to their campsite where Christine is a solitary figure framed by the campfire's smoke. Coming up behind her, Maury places his hands on his daughter's shoulders, and the two stand in silence with the heat of the fire on their faces and the chill of the late winter day on their backs.

Chapter 12

CONSTRUCTION BEGINS

Most of the season's workers are on site: two hundred families camped on five acres of frozen flat land that turns to ankle-deep mud most days when the sun shines. I sleep on a cot in the camp store and keep the fire in the Franklin going. Barnum, well rested from his overnight stay in the Jonesville Hotel, is on his way back up to Montreal to fetch the last bunch of doggers for the season's crew. My routine includes shoveling the snow and dried mud off the store deck, and helping to unload the supplies that come up from Northfield. Lucky doesn't do much more than wag is tail and smile with his tongue out, so comparatively, I'm being more useful.

Every time a new member of the crew asks me a question, it's easy to maintain my deafness. I just put my hands to my ears, shake my head, and bark, "Derf." He'd get an apologetic expression on his face and ask his question with hand gestures and talking louder, as if that is going to get through my deafness.

Sometimes I play with them. Of course I hear every word, but I pretend I don't understand until I light up with an expression of understanding and point them in the right direction. I get a kick out of that. You have to make your own fun whenever ya can under circumstances such as these.

I see a young girl hanging around the store, and motion her to come inside. Once inside she goes right over to the stove, and holds her hands up to the stove to warm them. I take a broom, motion it toward her, and say, "Seep?" She smiles and eagerly grabs it. "My name is Christine," she says.

I hold my hands up to my ears and shake my head. "Oh," she says, "Can't you hear?" I shake my head again. She looks around and finally motions me over to the counter. With her finger she writes out CHRISTINE in the dust, and pats her chest.

I smile and write "Dug" on the counter. My given name, Dubhghlas, is Gaelic. Christine smiles and out loud says, "Hello, Doug," and holds out her hand which I take and shake it vigorously. She starts to sweep.

Outside, the foremen are shouting orders. Most of the men on site are working the woods: felling trees, driving mules to drag the timber out to the worksite, stripping bark, and running the logs through a steam powered trench saw ripping them in half, or roughly squaring the logs for use as ties. The bark and branches are stockpiled to sell back to us for the campfires. Several men drive mules dragging dollies of squared timbers across the foot bridge to the other side of the river up past Catherine's boardinghouse, and leaving them alongside what will be the new rail bed.

Mr. Eggleston stands guard in front of Catherine's boardinghouse to assure no one is waylaid by the warmth and spirits inside. But Catherine doesn't tend her tavern during the day this time of year; she's busy trudging into the woods on snowshoes carrying in empty buckets and coming out with a yoke over her shoulders weighed down by the last buckets of sap tapped from the trees on the north side of the mountains behind her establishment. Thick clouds of steam rise from a kettle suspended over a fire behind her boardinghouse.

Eventually, the crew is divided into four groups. The timber crew is making ties and timbers for laying track and constructing the trestle. The rock crew is tasked with hauling rip-rap to serve as footings for the trestle. A small group is dragging ties across the footbridge to where the fourth crew is preparing the rail bed on the far side of the river.

This has been the routine for the last several weeks, not slowing for late winter snow or the rain that seems to be unending this year. What might have been cause for complaint under other circumstances is hardly noticed as the workers and their families feel the weight of oppression, famine, and hopelessness lifted from their daily lives. Around the campfires, the laughter and singing increase every night, and the season's rising temperatures give a hint that the cold and rain will likely give way to warmer days and nights. And though it rains quite a bit, there's hot food to be had each morning and night.

Every day here, except Sunday, is a full workday that begins shortly after sunrise and continues until a few minutes before evening supper. Sunday mornings are given over to rest or worship once the breakfast chores are done. We have two priests laboring in the camps this season, both refugees themselves, so we usually have two church services going simultaneously. Barker won't let Catherine join in, so most Sundays she and her husband ride to Jonesville – even in foul weather - where a Catholic service is held in the back of the general store.

We Irish are not accepted by the general population, and neither is our allegiance to the Pope. We arrive in need, mostly without resources and not in good health. But we are free to follow our faith even if we have to keep a low profile and occasionally endure ridicule and derision.

At this morning's service I stand next to Christine, the young lady I had met early on, and who helps me sweep the store. In fact, she shows up most days at the store to help. When she's done, she joins the other children, keeping an eye on the younger ones while their mothers do chores. Lately, I've noticed she will wait for her father to go into the woods and then goes across the bridge to Catherine's boardinghouse. At first she just sat on the porch watching the men work, but now I see she and Catherine have become acquainted, and they sit and talk for quite awhile before they both return to the tasks at hand.

After today's church service I make a point of walking with her as the crowd dispersed. I point to her, point to the store, make a sweeping motion, and bark, "Seep?"

She shakes her head, "No, sir," comes her reply as a smile brightens her face, and she points to Mrs. Dillon's establishment across the river. I couldn't tell if she forgot I'm deaf, or she simply feels free to talk, but she says, "I like Mrs. Dillon. I think she runs the boardinghouse all by herself. She has so many stories to tell. I like her, and I especially like the maple sap she's collecting. I think the dog likes the sap, too, because I saw him push his nose into an empty bucket trying to lick it clean, and once he pushed it all around the yard before Mrs. Dillon could catch him!"

Christine laughs, then looks concerned and says, "I think Mr. Dillon is ill. He sleeps quite a bit, and when he is awake, he doesn't do much to help Mrs. Dillon."

I want to make a comment about that lush of a man, but I, of course, can't. Truth is he imbibes as often as he takes a breath. In fact, his orneriness and constant drunkenness is the basis of what sympathy and tolerance the managers here have for Mrs. Dillon. Well, that, and she's a pleasure to look at. She can't be a day older than twenty years, and is tall, slender, with long curly blond hair down to her shoulders with all the womanly garments to please her customers at night. I admire her spunk and her ability to carve out a living in the wilderness. Quite a good living, too, I understand.

Christine continues talking, and I'm beginning to wonder who she's talking to. "Just this morning Mrs. Dillon told me how sometimes she has to go all the way into Canada to get some supplies, and on her way back she gets chased by men on horseback and sometimes she gets robbed! Can you imagine that?" Christine turns her head toward me and is wide-eyed and awe-struck.

I pretend I didn't hear her. Again I point to her, point to the store, make a sweeping motion, and bark, "Seep?"

Christine shakes her head and says, "Not today. Maybe later. Mrs. Dillon invited me to help her boil some more sap!" Hopping off the store porch, she turns and disappears into the crowd waiting for breakfast, heading toward her tent site. Later, while stacking wood outside the store, I see Christine cross the bridge, and as she is about to knock on the Dillon's door, it opens and Catherine appears in the open door. I go back to stacking wood.

Chapter 13

CATHERINE'S NEW FARMHAND

"Good morning, Christine. Come to help me?"

"Yes, Ma'am."

"I'm going to make syrup again today. The season's just about over, so I need you to keep an eye on the kettle while I gather the last of the sap buckets. I'll show you how to tell when the sap has turned to syrup."

"How do I do that?"

"Come on inside while I get my coat," says Catherine. The two disappear inside the tavern entrance. Christine looks about and sees two windows on the north wall facing the camp, and another on the west wall next to the side entrance. The three windows let in daylight to illuminate the room where she sees tables and chairs and a chest-high half log split lengthwise and supported at each end by wooden barrels. Behind the log was a long shelf, and on it were bottles of different shapes and colors. A Franklin stove heated the room.

"This looks like a tavern," says Christine.

"It is, dear. Along with renting rooms to boarders, this is also how we earn a living. For the past several years we've set up our boardinghouse along the Stage Road near the construction sites. We build, buy, or rent a new building each year, set it up over the winter, and open for business when the first workers arrive."

A gruff voice bellows from the back room, "Who's here, Kate? Who are you talking to?" Pushing open the door that separates the back room from the barroom, Mr. Dillon shuffles in and towers over Christine. A large man made larger by layers of heavy clothes, he is unshaven with unkempt dark bushy hair. "This is no place for a little girl. Git. Go outside."

Startled, Christine looks at Mrs. Dillon, then up at Mr. Dillon, and turns for the door. As Christine lifts the latch Mrs. Dillon says, "I'll be right out, Christine."

She could hear Mr. Dillon's voice raised, but couldn't quite hear Mrs. Dillon's replies. In a few minutes, Mrs. Dillon appears holding a large, long-handled metal feed scoop. "Now this is what you are going to use to know when the sap has turned to syrup. Come on, I'll show you!" Catherine leads Christine to an area behind the building where the snow is packed down from her syrup-making routine. A kettle releasing steam into the spring air is hanging from an iron tripod over the fire; a stack of split wood nearby.

"I need you to keep the fire going. Not too hot, but just hot enough to keep the sap boiling. Come here, I want to show you when you'll know the sap has turned to syrup." Catherine, scoop in hand, dips it into the cauldron. She holds it up over the kettle and starts moving the scoop side to side as she slowly returns the clear liquid to the kettle.

"See how the sap still runs out like water? I'm going to go collect more sap, and I want you to keep an eye on the fire. Remember, just add enough wood to keep it boiling," and she hangs the scoop on the tripod.

Christine nods and picks up a piece of wood. She stands up wind of the fire and watches Catherine follow her well-trodden path through the foot of snow still on the ground and into the woods carrying the yoke at her side with two buckets hanging from each end. After a few minutes, the wood on the fire settles, and Christine puts two more split logs on it. She peeks into the kettle to see the sap is still a-boil. The steam warms her face and fills her nose with a sweet aroma.

Catherine soon re-appears with the yoke bending over her shoulders. As she approaches the kettle, she kneels down, bents forward, and rests the four buckets full of clear sap on the ground, pushing the yoke over her head. She stands up and turns to Christine, "Now, watch this."

Taking the scoop, she dips it into the kettle and lets the sap run out again. This time it runs off the scoop like a shimmering golden curtain. It is thicker and darker than before. "When the sap runs back into the kettle without breaking up it'll form a sheet as you move the scoop back and forth. That's when you know it's turned to syrup. If you wait too long it'll harden into maple sugar when it cools. But we're going to take this off of the fire now and let the syrup cool in the snow."

Catherine puts on leather mittens laying nearby and hoists the kettle off of its hook and onto a small table. On the ground next to the table are more empty buckets, and Catherine gently tips the kettle and fills each bucket until the kettle is empty. She returns the kettle to the fire and pours the newly collected sap into the kettle.

Catherine pauses and turns her head toward Christine, "I have a treat for you," and she picks up one of the buckets with the warm syrup, takes a few steps into new snow, and pours a bit onto the snow in two spots. The warm syrup drills two holes in the snow and disappears.

Christine is wide-eyed, "What are you doing?"

"Come here." Catherine bends over and scoops her hand into the snow under one hole and pulls up a small golden crystal ball. She hands it to Christine and digs down for the second one. "That's a little treat for helping me today," and Catherine takes a bite of her ball of frozen maple sugar.

Christine holds it in her outstretched hand, letting the sun shine through the golden crystals. She brings it up to her lips and licks it; the sharp crystals quickly yielding to the heat of her tongue.

"Take a bite!" says Catherine.

Christine bites off a small piece that melts on her tongue and fills her mouth with maple sweetness. She takes another bite and giggles. "Oh, my! That's wonderful! What do you call it?"

"I've heard it called sugared snow. I'm glad you like it." Glancing back toward the woods, Catherine is pensive, "This'll be the last day we collect sap. The trees behind us are starting to bud, and even though this has been a late winter, even the trees high up on the north slope are losing their sweetness. I have four more buckets in the woods to bring down, and that will be the last of it." Catherine takes only the yoke on her return trip into the woods and returns with four half-full buckets. Christine tends the fire. As the final kettle is hoisted from the fire and disgorges its contents into the last of the empty buckets, Catherine suggests it's time for Christine to return to camp.

"May I come back tomorrow? I want to do more to help you."

Catherine pauses before answering. "You've been a great help, Christine, but are you sure your mother and father don't have chores for you to do?"

"No, ma'am. Mama died before we left home, and I don't have that much to do except help a man named Doug at the company store. It's just my Papa and me, and I get our chores done not long after Papa goes off to work, and then I might watch the younger children or I do some sewing. But, I don't have to work at the store, and I'd much rather help you…that is, if I'm not in your way."

Putting her hand on Christine's shoulder, "I'm sorry to hear about your mother, dear. No, you won't be in my way. You be certain to ask your father if it's all right for you to come and help me. If he is agreeable, you can help me start this year's garden, and if you help me with the chickens I'll give you a fresh egg everyday you help me."

Hearing that, Christine's face brightens. She wants to hug Catherine, but thinks the better of it. "Oh, yes! I'm sure Papa will want me to help you!" Christine yelled back over her shoulder, "I'll see you tomorrow." She heads toward the footbridge as the daylight fades and the sky shows the pinks of the setting sun. Slogging through the mix of snow and mud, Christine returns to their campsite where Mrs. O'Reilly is tending the campfire.

Soon Maury returns with Patrick, and the two make their way to the food line, small pails in hand. Many of the fires throughout the encampment now have a ring of stumps or rough hewn benches encircling each. Maury and Patrick return to their site placing their pails on several stumps and sitting on others. Patrick and Maury talk mostly about the dangers of working in the woods. Christine is waiting for a lull in the conversation to tell about her day, but before she can jump it, her father turns to her, "Christine, did I see you across the river with Mrs. Dillon?"

"Oh, yes, Papa! Ms. Dillon taught me how to boil sap to make syrup, and then she poured some syrup on the snow, and it was the sweetest thing I have ever tasted! She said if I come back and help her with her garden and her chickens she would give me a fresh egg everyday!"

"I don't want you to be spending a lot of time with Mr. and Mrs. Dillon. That's not the kind of place for a young lady. I suppose helping

Mrs. Dillon with chores will be fine, if, and only if, your chores here in camp are done. Is that understood?"

"Yes, Papa."

Christine took pleasure in setting up their new home; organizing their tent's contents and washing clothes in the small brook at the east end of the flats with the other ladies. Two days passed before she ventured back across the footbridge. Neither Catherine nor her husband is to be seen as she approaches the house. In the camps behind her, there's a constant symphony of sound as the valley holds in the echoes of barked orders mixed with the intermittent crack of felled trees and the rhythmic percussion of ax on wood. Christine walks past the now cold kettle at the rear of the house to where Catherine is dressing a deer. It hangs upside down with its belly open and blood draining into a bucket.

Catherine catches a glimpse of Christine approaching, and her face brightens as she pauses in her work, "Good morning, Christine! Have you come to help me today, or is this just a social visit?"

"I've come to help, if there's something I can do."

"Yes, yes. Come on back to the coop, and bring that bucket," says Catherine pointing to a bucket by the shed door. Christine hoists the bucket full of grain with both hands, and it bangs her knees as she carries it to the chicken coop. "It's nice to see you again. I missed you yesterday," says Catherine. "I saw this buck licking one of the trees I had tapped, so I fetched my gun and here he is. I could have used your help dragging him out of the woods."

Christine felt a twinge of guilt. "Didn't Mr. Dillon help you?" Her question went unanswered. "Well, now that we're settling in, Papa wants me to make camp more of a home, and I've been helping out Doug at the company store, too, so... And...," her voice trails off.

"And?"

"Papa did say that he doesn't want me to spend too much time here, but he said I could help you with chores. So here I am. To help."

"I'm very happy to see you. Here's a rake, and I'd like you to start by pulling all of the soiled bedding out of the coop and putting it on the ground between the square marked with stakes over there. That'll be our garden. Then take some new hay from a bail in the shed and replace the bedding you remove. When you're done, get a basket out of the kitchen so you can gather eggs."

Delighted, Christine grabs the rake and heads into the coop. Catherine returns her attention to the inverted deer. Catherine's gaze follows Christine as she makes the trek from the coop to the garden and back again and again. After awhile Christine emerges from the coop bristling with hay all up and down her frock with some stuck in her hair. She walks over to where Catherine is now kneeling in the snow, skinning the deer. "I'm ready to collect eggs, Mrs. Dillon."

Catherine turns and looks up. Pulling pieces of hay from Christine's hair, "Ha! My! You're wearing quite a bit of that hay, Christine!" Catherine pauses as Christine starts to brush herself off. "How old are you, Christine?"

"I'll be fourteen in July."

"Hm-m. Fourteen. You're becoming a young lady. Are you finished with your schooling?"

"Oh, no, ma'am. Papa says when we settle down, I'm to return to my studies because I want to be a teacher. But I haven't had school for more than a year, and I miss it a lot."

"I think I should have a talk with your father. Will you ask him to meet me at the footbridge after supper tonight?"

"Yes, ma'am. I'll ask him."

Mr. Dillon had come from the cabin and is standing behind Catherine. He grabs Catherine by the arm, stands her up, and turns her around. "What's going on here? Who are you meeting tonight?"

"I want to get Christine's father's permission to help me with the chickens. That'll be one less thing you have to do, Shamus."

Shamus releases his wife and turns toward the cabin. He struggles to make his feet step into the tracks he had just made through the snow that remains from the long winter. He stops, hesitates, and turns back to Christine and Catherine. "Yeah, OK, you tell him I want to talk to him, too."

With her brow furled Christine looks at Catherine. Catherine puts her hand on Christine's shoulder, "You can ignore him. In five minutes he won't remember he said that. Tell your Papa that I would like to speak with him so I can put his mind at ease. In the meantime, here's a little something for helping me." And Catherine hands Christine two fresh eggs.

Chapter 14

PAYDAY

I see Christine go back and forth to Catherine's boardinghouse just about everyday, always comin' back before sunset and before the men finish their day's work. Some time ago I was standing nearby when I overheard Mr. Murphy askin' his daughter what kinds of chores she was doing across the river at the boardinghouse and his concerns about her spending time there, but I couldn't say anything to him because, well, because I'm deaf. What I did do was touch Mr. Murphy's arm, motion over my shoulder to the boardinghouse, and with a thumb up I nodded so vigorously my hat fell off. Mr. Murphy seemed to get the message: Christine's in good hands with Catherine. Her husband's another story, but I didn't know how to get that across.

Today's a big day. It's the end of April and word's gotten out that the month's payroll is on the way. Even the supervisors are lookin' forward to it – the first payroll of the year for the full crew. The supervisor's got their first pay of the year last month when the season started. At the morning muster the crews gather outside the store, and the supervisors make the assignments for the day. Finally, Barnum ends by telling everyone to return to the store at the end of the day, and payroll will be distributed. With that a great shout goes up, and the crews seem to work especially hard all day until daylight starts to fade, and the anticipation of getting their first wages becomes a distraction.

Right on schedule, Mr. Ferris, the county sheriff, appears at the end of the day, his pudgy face framed by tussled hair unable to be confined by his hat, and a bushy beard which, on this occasion, carries a remnant of a meal taken earlier in the day. It's not unusual to see the sheriff here on a payday because, as he says, he's responsible for patrolling the boardinghouse. In truth, he uses it as an excuse to shake down any crew that might have too much to drink, and to be near Catherine, even though she makes her dislike of him known at every opportunity. The sheriff appears to be what we call "Black Irish." Likely, his ancestors migrated to the Emerald Isle from the Iberian Peninsula generations ago. He never has said what town or county he's from, but he's mentioned that he came from Ireland five or six years ago and smart enough to leave before the latest famine had taken hold. Short of stature with dark hair, dark eyes, and an unwarranted swagger, he's not a man of high character.

A few weeks ago I heard him tell Catherine that the he is enforcing a new license law. He said she must have a license in order for her to sell liquor and to collect taxes, but I heard her tell him right back that she was granted a tavern license by the state of Vermont, and as far as collecting and paying liquor taxes, that was a matter between her and the state, having nothing to do with a county sheriff. Ferris didn't have anything to say in return, so she must have it straight.

Just about everyone around here, including the sheriff, knows Catherine smuggles in most of her liquor from Canada. Down south, the Commonwealth of Massachusetts has always had strong laws keeping a man from his drink, and the State of Maine is even stricter, so she heads north. It's closer, and if she manages to avoid paying import duties, then all the better for her and her customers. Oh, yes, it's true: she's been caught several times from the stories she tells, but she's clever enough to know how to cooperate with the authorities at the border, and I've heard she isn't above bribing the law, and maybe even a judge or two. But you didn't hear that from me because I don't know that to be the case – just stories told every now and then among the supervisors.

The only authority she won't cooperate with is Ferris. He makes advances on her when Shamus isn't around or passed out, but she'll have none of it. She has a thirteen-bore single barrel flintlock long gun I've seen her point at the man to send him on his way, and she can use it, too. She hunts and usually has plenty of dried, smoked, or salted meat to be washed down by the spirits she sells. The salted turkey is my favorite.

This evening there's a lot of laughing and loud talk among the men gathered outside the store. Inside the store Lucky and I are with the supervisors, including General Manager Belknap and Sheriff Ferris. Belknap asks for everyone's attention, "Gentlemen, listen, please. I started up with the Company's payroll last week, stopping in Northfield, Barre, and Waterbury. I was instructed to pay our creditors along the way, and to pay you and the crew with the rest. Trouble is, there was not enough to pay our suppliers all that we owe and have enough remaining for the full payroll."

"What about us?" asks Eggleston. "Are we getting paid? It's been a month."

"Yes, you'll all get paid most of what's due, but there's only enough for forty cents on the dollar for each of the men outside, so this is what we are going to do."

He turns to Barnum, "I want you to go out and announce the men are to start work as usual in the morning, and we'll call 'em in alphabetically. Then we'll settle payroll one by one. That's exactly what I want you to say, 'to settle payroll.' Then as each man comes in we'll look at the ledger and deduct his store account from his wages. If we owe him money, we'll tell him he has a credit at the store. If anyone makes a fuss we'll give him half of the balance due in cash. Any questions?"

Ferris brightens and puts his hands to the two pistols he keeps in his belt, "Do you want me here in case there's trouble?"

"No, I do not, Sheriff," says Belknap. "This is our business, and there won't be any trouble. Any other questions?"

"Boss," says Barnum, "Is this going to be like last year?" referring to the short payrolls toward the end of last season.

"Not likely, George. The board has assessed the shareholders, and from what I was told, the assessments are coming in. We just owed a little bit more than we expected to the suppliers because of the additional crew. Workers can be replaced, but there's no substitute for food, lumber, and rails.

"Anything else?" asks Belknap.

Of course it was going to be like last year. They didn't provide full payroll for the crews toward the end of the year, and the Board never did pay the balance due before the workers were dispersed and abandoned. A lot of the shareholders won't be able to pay their share assessments, and it'll be up to the board members to buy up their shares or watch the share value drop. They won't accept promises to pay from the common shareholders, but some of the Board members can give promises to pay for the shares they want to buy. The banks don't consider our shares or the board members' promises sound enough to be collateral for additional loans, so cash is short and probably getting shorter. We're half way to Burlington from Northfield, and some of the major investors are running out of cash.

The next morning, sure enough, the men are told, one by one and in small groups that instead of getting all of the cash due, their store balance is being paid, and the rest of the wages owed are going to be paid with store credit. At first, only a few had strong objections, and those who strongly protested did leave the store with some cash. But when word got out that demanding cash would get you some pay, the cash ran out before all of the M's made it into the store. Since most of us here are Irish, many M's went unpaid, and the O's got nothing.

After Mr. Murphy left the store, empty-handed, I see him head toward the footbridge, and I follow several paces behind. We cross the river and head to the tavern. Mr. Murphy opened the door and holds it for me. I tip my hat and enter. There are several men standing at the bar, Shamus is at a table, and Catherine is working behind the bar with Mr. Strong, the blacksmith from Jonesville. When Catherine is anticipating a busy night, and the first payday of the season is sure to be a busy night, she has Mr. Strong come and help serve.

Catherine notices Maury walk in and, wiping her hands on her apron, she approaches him and says, "Oh, Mr. Murphy, thank you for coming. Let's talk outside."

Maury turns and walks out, standing just off the steps outside the door. Catherine follows him out wearing a dress with a lacy blouse cut low and cinched at her waist emphasizing her feminine figure. She wore a shawl and draped it over her shoulders clutching it tightly under her chin.

"Mr. Murphy…"

"Christine said you wanted to talk to me, Mrs. Dillon," Maury says, looking around to see who might be watching. Shamus stickks his head

out the open door, hesitates, looks like he was going to say something, but then retreats back inside.

"Yes, I do, Mr. Murphy. I know a boardinghouse that serves liquor is no place for a young lady, but I want you to know this is also my home. I hunt, trap, tap maple trees, raise chickens, and have a garden that keeps us well fed throughout the year. I run a boardinghouse with rooms above the tavern as our main business, but I would never have Christine do anything that involves the tavern."

"Well, I know, but...."

"She told me that she lost her mother, and she seems to enjoy helping me with my chores. God knows my husband isn't any help, so I could use an extra hand, and I think I can also help Christine...help Christine become a woman."

Maury, worried that he won't be able to raise Christine properly after her mother's passing, he is touched by Catherine's words. Christine is, indeed, becoming a woman, and he's busy each day with work, and the only schooling available at camp is for children much younger than Christine. Catherine is offering to play a role in Christine's up-bringing that he is finding difficult to provide.

"I appreciate your interest in my daughter, Mrs. Dillon. She means the world to me, and I just want to make certain she is safe and not exposed to the vulgar side of life. We have both suffered heartache, and the loss of her mother and brother to the famine was a terrible thing for her to experience. She's smart and ambitious, and I want her to learn those things that will prepare her for her new life."

"Mr. Murphy, this is..."

He interrupts, "Please call me Maury."

Catherine pauses, seeing Maury, a sincerely caring father, in a new light, "Thank you, Maury, and please call me Catherine." Here is a man taking action to improve his lot in life and showing concern for his daughter, she thinks. He seems to have a higher character than most others.

"Maury, this is a new world; very different than the Old World. I will treat Christine as if she were my own daughter. She is beautiful and full of a desire for learning new things. She said she would like to be a teacher, and I think she would be a wonderful teacher. But first you and she have to survive this construction season. I will take good care of her while you're working. She can help me with my chores and learn some things along the way."

Maury is listening, but Catherine's grip on her shawl had relaxed, and Maury is distracted by the low cut of Catherine's blouse. How long had it been…? The loss of his wife and son, his entire community suffering the famine, and the task of procuring passage to North America had consumed his attention for the last several years. Now he could not help but to be drawn to the woman standing before him. Strawberry blond hair touching Catherine's shoulders; her smooth skin disappearing into the fold of her breasts becoming more exposed by the loosening grip on her shawl. "Yes. All right. I did appreciate the eggs you gave Christine, and she is very fond of you. You are very generous."

"She earned those eggs for helping me with the chickens."

"Yes, and…," Maury's eyes couldn't resist drifting down again to glance at those parts of Catherine that were increasingly uncovered. Catherine drops her head down to catch Maury's focus, and laughs, bringing his gaze back to her sparkling green eyes. Catherine smiles, puts her warm hand on Maury's arm, and comes a half step closer. Looking up and speaking reassuringly, "We both have the best interests of Christine at heart."

"Yes. I can see that. If Christine can be of help to you, then I approve. I know she is fond of you and enjoys doing the chores you have given her," he says returning Catherine's smile. "Frankly, Catherine, I'm not sure I can keep her away."

"Then it's settled. I have a new farmhand, and you'll see I will take good care of her." Catherine's hand stays on Maury's arm, and a wordless moment passes, then another. Her hand drops, and she steps back, pulling her shawl up over her shoulders.

"Yes, well… I'm glad we had this talk," says Maury. "I'll let Christine know she is welcome to come help you during the day and is to return to the camp before dark." He wants to say more, but instead hears himself say, "Well, good evening, Mrs. Dillon… Catherine." Maury tips his hat as he backs away and returns to camp where Christine is waiting.

"Papa, what did Mrs. Dillon want to talk to you about?"

"We talked about you helping her, and I told her you could, but only during daylight hours and only after your chores at our camp are done."

"Oh, good!" says Christine, throwing her arms around her father and kissing his cheek. "She's very nice. It'll be wonderful!! You'll see."

Maury hadn't seen Christine this happy and excited in several years. Certainly not since her mother passed, and, really, not since the famine started to take hold in '43.

Chapter 15

FULL SWING

Catherine comes back inside as I watch Mr. Murphy cross the river and return to camp. Mr. Dillon meets her at the door and grabs Catherine's elbow. He speaks in a whisper, but with an intensity that seems threatening. I can't hear what is being said, but Catherine soon pulls her arm away and pushes him toward the back room.

I slap a dime on the counter, and Catherine fills a glass with hard cider. She looks at me. Leaning forward, and not more than six inches from my supposedly deaf self she says in a whisper, "I'm done with that man, and I have a plan." Standing back up and glancing around at the other patrons, "Who's next?"

What the hell was that all about? Does she know I can hear, or does she think her plan is safe with me because I'm deaf? Either way, her secret is safe with me. But a plan? This should be good.

Lucky and I mill around the tavern filled with men the rest of the evening. There's a lot of complaining, but wasn't nothin' they could do about it. They're stuck. They have shelter and food which is more than most of 'em had when they were recruited at the dock, so they're going to stay on, and they're going back to work tomorrow.

When tomorrow came I couldn't help but notice something out of the ordinary. Usually, when Mrs. Dillon leaves the site she heads west in her buckboard, but at first light this morning I saw her on horseback at a full gallop heading east on the Stage Road toward Waterbury. It wasn't until afternoon that she returned, and empty handed, too, or at least it appeared that way.

For the last several years we've been laying track east to west through Washington County, but this season we've crossed into Chittenden County. Most of Catherine's permits from now on will come from the west, so I can't figure what her interest might be east of here. That woman never ceases to surprise me… or management. To think how an immigrant woman without much help, if any, could establish and run such a boardinghouse year after year and defend her business against the efforts of the railroad was hard to imagine. Mrs. Dillon is a remarkable woman.

Now that we're five weeks into the season there's a certain amount of routine around camp; that's why seeing Catherine gallop off this morning grabbed my attention. What's also different these days is the construction of the trestle is about to start. The loggers have stockpiled green timbers stripped of their bark and ripped in half, and the mules have started dragging boulders to the bank to roll into the river for footings as each bent is sited.

I heard discussions among the supervisors that the last trestle they built used fully milled timbers for each bent, and they had their doubts about using un-milled timbers this year. The way they described it, each bent was assembled on the bank with the joints and cross bracing secured by large bolts. As each bent was built and placed in the river, one after another, stringers were placed from one bent to next, and secured with large bolts and washers until the river was crossed.

The company's engineer, Mr. Stoughton, came up by train a few days ago to supervise construction. He picked out a site well upriver from where this year's trestle will be, and he and Mr. Eggleston and Mr. Freeman have driven stakes into the ground to guide the construction of each bent. This is what he told the half circle of trestle crew, four men deep, as several experienced workers assembled the first bent:

"We've laid out a jig by putting stakes in the ground so that each bent will be the exactly the same. Each bent has two inner support posts that are vertical, and two outer posts, each with a slight inward lean." The workers laid the four vertical posts, both about sixteen feet long and sharpened at one end, in between the stakes in the ground.

Mr. Stoughton continued, "Each bent will have a sill at the top and four sway braces spiked into the verticals. The sharp ends will sink into the river bed." The men took a milled piece of timber from a nearby stack and spiked it into the top of the four logs already in place. They then placed four long planks on the long posts forming one X above the other and drove spikes into each place where the planks crossed a log.

"Once a bent is completed four ropes will be tied on each side, here and here," as he pointed to the top and middle of the bent laying on the ground, "and the whole assembly will be pushed into the river and floated down to where it will be raised to vertical and secured in place. The first bent will be secured to the bank by two timbers; one end notched and spiked into the cap, and the other spiked to a log pile buried in the granite approach," he said pointing to the top of the partially assembled bent laying on the ground then to the stumps sunk into the carefully laid granite apron on the bank.

"The second bent will be mated to the first forming a double bent. Each double bent will be secured using four stringers attaching one double bent to the next pair. Two stringers will be attached midway up the posts and two more at the top. I will be here to see the first two double bents are properly placed, and Mr. Eggleston and Mr. Freeman will be the site supervisors from that point on." Mr. Stoughton smiled, patted Mr. Freeman on his back, and made his way to the store.

I watched the whole demonstration remembering Mr. Stoughton's presentation of this construction method at the board meeting. He said it was going to be a way to save time and money.

I return to the store and am there when Mr. Belknap tells Barnum several board members will be coming up to inspect our progress, but he doesn't know when. Seems the board expects the trestle to be completed by the end of May, but Belknap expresses his doubts they can meet that deadline for completing the trestle. But, work on the rail bed leading up to the trestle is progressing, and construction of the bed on the south side of the river is beginning in earnest, right on schedule.

As spring weather takes hold, the days are getting longer, but it's still raining more days than not. Normally, there'd be less mud to contend with, but on the bright side, the days and nights are getting warmer. After five or six weeks of work, life in the camps has taken on a rhythm, and each crew has composed its own cadence. Catherine's boardinghouse has a steady business both from workers who have cash to spend and a growing number of travelers using the Stage Road.

Chapter 16

WHAT'S GOING ON HERE?

The last drops of rain are falling from the day's gray sky as Catherine lights the tavern lanterns to beckon workers from across the river. I start across the footbridge just behind Mr. Murphy and Mr. O'Reilly when our attention is drawn to Sheriff Ferris, Catherine, and her husband in an animated discussion outside the tavern. Mr. Murphy breaks into a trot when he sees Catherine has Christine behind her, seemingly shielding Christine from the two men. I hurry my pace as Patrick quickens his.

Maury approaches and stands next to Catherine keeping Christine behind them both.

"I don't trust her, walkin' in and out of my house as she pleases, and she's stealing eggs from the henhouse, " says Shamus pointing an accusing finger at Christine cowering behind Mr. Murphy and Catherine.

Ferris pulls on his beard, "If she's stealing from you, Mr. Dillon, then I might have to…."

Catherine cuts him off mid-sentence, "You're not going to do a damned thing, Sheriff. I hired Christine to help me with chores." Catherine steps aside and places her arm around Christine's shoulder, urging her to come out from behind her father. As Christine brings her eyes up from the ground to face the sheriff the expression on her face changes from surprise to fear, and she quickly drops her gaze, and turns her face away from the sheriff, still standing between Catherine and her father.

"Now, isn't that a cozy site, Shamus?" says the sheriff taunting the poor creature.

Maury looks down at Christine, as she again retreats behind her father burying her face in the back of his coat. "That'll be enough, Sheriff," says Mr. Murphy.

"You don't get it, Mick. I'm the law here, and you immigrants don't have any rights. You don't get to talk back. I may have to lock up that young lady if Mr. Dillon here makes a complaint. What about it, Shamus, has that girl been stealing from you? She's acting kinda guilty."

Catherine steps forward, pushes Shamus aside, and approaches Ferris, "Leave us alone, Sheriff. You shouldn't rely on what he says. He's been drinking all day. I'm telling you she works for me, and she hasn't stolen anything."

"I can see what's going on here, Mrs. Dillon, and if your husband was half a man he would put a stop to it. But since he isn't, I'll let it go."

Shamus probably thought the Sheriff was still talkin' about the young girl stealing eggs, but it was clear to the rest of us that the sheriff is implying Catherine and Mr. Murphy have more than a passing interest in one another. Ferris mounts his horse, and delivers his parting comment as he set off down the Stage Road toward Jonesville, "You'd better keep a tight rein on your wife, Shamus."

"Come inside, Shamus, it's time to go to work," says Catherine as she turns her husband and pushes him toward the roadhouse. Maury looks down at Christine and sees she is almost in tears. "It's all right, Christine. The sheriff is full of himself and just likes to stir up trouble."

She hugged her father tightly and says, "I don't like him. I'm afraid of him. Papa, I think he…"

Still irritated by the sheriff's threats, Maury says, "I don't want to hear anymore, Christine. He's the sheriff, but you don't have anything to fear. Now, come on, it's getting late and time for bed."

As Patrick and Maury turn to return to camp, Christine runs ahead without looking back. I hear O'Reilly say, "That's one son of a bitch."

"Which one, Pat?" They both laugh. "That damned sheriff," says Patrick.

I turn away, and continue my mission to patronize the tavern. Inside two workers are seated at a table in the corner of the room, and I approach the bar near Catherine and her husband. "Shamus, this Saturday I want to get some supplies in White River Junction. We can take the train from Northfield, spend the night in White River Junction, and come back up Sunday." Shamus has no response either way, so I guess that's settled.

A few days later, early in the morning, I see Shamus and Catherine, bags packed, head off in the direction of Northfield atop their buckboard where they can catch the passenger train to take them the forty miles to White River Junction. It wasn't unusual for folks to take a short trip on the cars now that the railroads are snaking into the North Country. What would normally take ten hours in a buckboard now takes two hours by train. A smoother ride, too.

The next day, as evening approaches, Barnum and I are working in the store, and I see a carriage tied up to the hitching post in front of the boardinghouse. I scratch my head upon seeing Sheriff Wilbur, the Washington County Sheriff, sittin' on the tavern porch. It's kinda odd because it's Sunday and the tavern is closed for the day; the Dillons are still out of town, and we're no longer in the sheriff's County. Eggleston is overseeing the crew working that side of the river and occasionally goes over to chat with the sheriff. They know each other from past construction seasons in Washington County. Sheriff Wilbur is not at all like Sheriff Ferris. In fact, Wilbur and the Dillons are good friends, and he was always welcome in the Dillon's tavern. Sheriff Wilbur, in fact, is quite a musician, and in past seasons he would appear at the Dillon's to play a ditty or two on his fiddle or pipe. But this is the first time I've seen him up here this season.

Less than an hour later I see Catherine and her husband in their buckboard coming up the Stage Road, and Sheriff Wilbur and Eggleston stand to meet them. I nudge Barnum and point across to what's happening across the river. As Shamus unloads their bags from their buckboard, the sheriff takes one bag away from Shamus, puts it on the porch, opens it up, looks at its contents, and closes it. The sheriff and Shamus get into what looks like a heated discussion, and finally, the sheriff places the bag he was inspecting in his carriage, puts Mr. Dillon in irons, and has him sit in the back of the carriage facing the rear. Without looking back, Mrs. Dillon climbs up on her buckboard and pulls it around behind the boardinghouse as Sheriff Wilbur drives off toward Waterbury with his bewildered prisoner sitting in the back.

Mrs. Dillon comes around from behind the boardinghouse leading a saddled horse and leans against the hitching post, arms crossed, as she watches her husband looking shocked, baffled, and completely stripped of any dignity being tossed from side to side as Sheriff Wibur's carriage disappears around the bend. A few minutes later Catherine mounts and sets off at a slow pace east.

Sweet Mother of Jesus, what was that all about? I follow Barnum as he heads out of the store and across the river, and Lucky falls in behind.

Barnum, watching Mrs. Dillon heading east, saunters over to Eggleston, "What just happened here, Jonathan? Where's the sheriff taking Mr. Dillon?"

"From what I heard, Mr. Dillon couldn't find his valise when they got off the train in Northfield, so Catherine suggested he take another bag to trade when they find his. The sheriff arrested him for stealing the bag and took him off to jail."

Barnum looks puzzled. He lifts his hat and with the same hand scratches his head, "That's the damnedest thing! The sheriff got here pretty quick! How'd he know?" If he is expecting an answer, none is forthcoming. Turning to Eggleston, "Call the men in for the day."

Daylight is fading as the sun starts its slide behind the mountains. I follow Barnum as he returns to camp, and Lucky, too, returns to camp perhaps knowing there would be no business at the tavern tonight.

A crew laying railroad track near Danville, Vermont, circa 1846.

Typical wood trestle design. Iron bridges replaced
wooden trestles once the railroad was in operation and able to
transport the needed materials.

Chapter 17

BEST LAID PLANS

With night dropping on the valley Mr. Stoughton's in the store along with Belknap, Barker, and Eggleston as I help serve supper to the families still eating from the company's kettle. Instead of washing out the pots and ladles, I go inside to keep abreast of current events while I put up the last of the provisions recently delivered.

Mr. Stoughton is standing and pacing, stroking his close-cropped beard. "The men have made a good start on the trestle. So, I'm going to head back south, but I'll be back up with some of the board members when they come to check on your progress."

"That's never a good thing," Barker snickers looking at Eggleston, unmindful that Stoughton might not share his feelings. "All they do is find fault, and most of them treat us like field hands. If it weren't for us none of this would get done."

Mr. Stoughton doesn't take the bait, "Keep twelve men on the bank constructing the bents. The jig we laid out is working well, but I'd like to see another jig next to it so we can have a bent under construction at any given time. Lay out the second jig by laying a completed bent on the ground and driving in stakes around it. Assign six men to construct each bent, and six more are needed to move the bents into the river; four to rope each bent into place; and four more to raise 'em into position. Barker, do you have the list of men fit for construction?"

Barker nods, "We have a good crew this year. Two blacksmiths, a civil engineer, and more than twenty carpenters."

Eggleston, always eager to please, is writing down the numbers and adding them up, "So, you'll need twenty-six men?"

Stoughton turns toward him, "That's just to get started. Once the first bent is up and secured to the bank, and the second bent is being erected, we'll need to have at least four men moving milled timbers to the top of the bents and six men up on the bents ready with stringers and braces to tie the bents together.

Eggleston keeps writing, " So that's thirty men on shore, and six on the trestle."

"Each time a bent is moved into place have four more up top to secure the stringers. Each double bent will be five feet apart, and the river is a hundred and sixty feet across, so we'll need thirty-three bents. When the trestle is about halfway across I expect the bracing and stringers will have been completed and you can stop adding crew to the trestle."

Eggleston is obviously enjoying all his calculations, "So, let's see, if we add four men starting with the second bent, and stop adding men when…"

Stoughton interrupts Eggleston, "We'll have a maximum of forty men working in trestle, and thirty on shore supporting construction. We should be able to get at least two double bents in place each day, rain or shine, so the trestle should be up by early June and the ties and rails in place shortly thereafter." Stoughton looks at each man with a big grin, as if the job's already done. "Questions? Concerns?"

Belknap, rubbing his chin, looks pained, "I don't know about using un-milled timber for the bents. And, you're sure it'll hold if the braces are spiked instead of bolted?" Stoughton, apparently irritated by the question, is quick to respond, "Yes….certainly. Certainly. We'll fortify the trestle before it gets much use."

Chapter 18

A NORTH WOODS DIVORCE

A light rain starts to fall as I follow Mr. Barker leaving the store with his list of crew in hand. As he makes his way among the tents he repeats, "Trestle crew, go find Mr. Eggleston by the river after the morning meal." He stops at Patrick's tent, "O'Reilly?"

Patrick sticks his head out the flaps, "Yes, sir?"

"You said you were a civil engineer?"

"Yes, sir."

"I want you to find Mr. Eggleston in the morning over by the jigs for the bents. Tell him I sent you, and you've built bridges. He'll tell you what he wants you to do."

"Well, sir, I'd be glad to do that. What am I going to be doing?"

"With your experience, you are most likely going to be helping oversee trestle construction."

"Yes, sir. Can I expect to be earning a bit more than fifty cents a day?"

"You can do what you're told to do and get paid for a day's work, or you can quit. Your choice." Barker continues to move among the tents repeating, "Trestle crew meet Mr. Eggleston by the river after breakfast."

I'm getting unpleasantly wet following Barker, and almost bumped into Mr. Murphy who had come out of his tent when he heard Mr. O'Reilly talking to Barker. I stopped in my tracks, smiled, and tipped my hat. After returning my hat to its perch I turn away from the pair, look about aimlessly, and become invisible.

Patrick says, "Now that doesn't seem right. You pay a man the same whether he's moving crushed stone, or applying his education as an engineer to build a trestle? I have half a mind to quit. I hear there's a woolen mill just north of Burlington that pays a dollar a day for mechanics."

Looking about aimlessly, I see Mr. Murphy put his hand on O'Reilly's shoulder, "They won't let you leave if you owe them money on account, and even if you don't owe 'em anything, you're not going to get the pay they owe you if you leave. And you don't know if they need any help at the mill. Look at it this way, better to help supervise construction than hauling timber or swinging an adze all day."

"Ya got that right, but, still, seems like they're takin' every advantage of our misery they can. And we just let 'em."

"Come on, Patrick. Let's head over to the Catherine's, and I'll buy you a nip."

Patrick's eyes widen and a smile appears, "Aye, now that's a fine idea! I feel better already. Let's go!"

Maury sticks his head back into the tent and says in a whisper, "Christine, it's almost time to go to sleep. Mr. O'Reilly and I are going across the river, and I'll be back shortly. If you need anything, see Mrs. O'Reilly."

Patrick has a head start, so Mr. Murphy quickens his pace to catch up. I debate what I should do next, but the thought of enjoying the conviviality of Catherine's is more appealing than following Barker slogging among the tents in the rain. So I fall in line a half dozen paces behind Mr. Murphy and O'Reilly.

"I'll tell ya, Maury, that Catherine is one fine woman. Even if she didn't serve whiskey, I'd find any excuse to spend time in her company." O'Reilly turns to look at Maury who has caught up to his friend. If Mr. Murphy had a response, I didn't hear it.

O'Reilly adds, " 'Course, I'm a married man, but you…. You're free to do more than just look, my friend!"

"Mrs. Dillon has a husband, Patrick. I wouldn't…. Well, enough said."

A full moon blurred by rain clouds barely lights their way across the footbridge toward the tavern's warm glow. Light from the partially open door glistens on muddy ground. Barker and Barnum are out in front and stop talking as we approach. "Good evening, gentlemen," says Mr. Murphy, but he got only a nod in return. I tip my hat as I pass.

Inside, the stove is warm, and three or four men sit at each table. Maury and Patrick join two others standing at the bar. Catherine, leaning over the bar asks, "What can I get you, Mr. Murphy?"

"We're going to do a little celebrating with some whiskey, Mrs. Dillon," says Maury as he reaches into his pocket extracting two coins he slaps on the bar. Catherine fills two small glasses to the brim and places a glass of spring water next to each. Catherine's gaze falls on me as I hold up one finger, then hold my two hands in front of me, one palm up and the other above it palm down, six inches apart signifying a tankard, willing to let Catherine decide if it will be hard cider or ale. Catherine must be feeling generous, because she hands me a tankard of ale and pushes my coin back to me. I tip my hat, bow slightly, and take my drink to the far end of the bar where I lean against the wall so I can take in the entire room.

Catherine's sparkling eyes stay fixed on Maury, "What are you gentlemen celebrating?" Catherine is standing tall with her hair up, loosely tied in back, and white lace ruffles bordering the bodice of a low cut dress emphasizing that she is, indeed, an attractive young woman. From the talk around camp, she attracts more business in her summer dresses, and that certainly seems to be her strategy tonight.

Patrick replies, "We're celebrating the fact that I've been promoted!" He takes a drink. "Yup. I've been promoted! More responsibility with no more pay. Reminds me of home." He and Maury both laugh and take another sip. "Certainly seems to hold true that those who got gets, and those who don't got don't get." Raising his glass in an imaginary toast, Patrick takes another sip.

"Patrick," says Maury, "We can celebrate our arrival in the New World and finally gettin' a foothold in the American States." Holding his glass toward Patrick, they touch glasses and empty them both. Maury turns to step away from the bar, and Catherine refills their glasses. "Oh, no, Mrs. Dillon. One's my limit tonight."

"This one's on the house, Mr. Murphy. I'm doing a bit of celebrating myself."

"Yes? And why would that be, Mrs. Dillon?" Maury asks, glad to have a reason to stay longer.

"Perhaps you heard that my husband was arrested," she says.

Patrick is quick to reply, "Why no," feigning ignorance of the series of events that had made the round of the camps. "Is that what's happened?" Of course the whole camp knew he had been arrested, but the reason why and the details varied greatly. "We did see that he went off with the sheriff. Why was he arrested? What did he do?"

"Yes, well, we were returning from a trip, and when we disembarked his valise was nowhere to be found. So I suggested Mr. Dillon take another bag to trade for his when his is found. Low and behold, the sheriff from Washington County got wind of what happened, and arrested him for stealing the bag."

"That's quite a tale, Mrs. Dillon. But what are you celebrating?" asks Patrick. Maury is spell bound and speechless, but listening intently.

"Well, Mr. Dillon was put on trial the next day, and found guilty. The judge gave him the choice of five years in prison or ten years in the federal army," Catherine says. "So, he chose to join the army, and I understand he's being sent to the western territories – Indian country. Perhaps the army will sober him up."

"Well, that's the damnedest story, Mrs. Dillon," says Patrick. "How are you going to manage without him?"

"I expect I'll manage better without him! He was no help, and he drank most of the profits. I think he and I are both going to be better off this way," she says, winking at Maury. Catherine resumes wiping the bar and moves down to serve the other customers.

"What do you make of that, Maury?" asks O'Reilly. "I mean, how the hell did the sheriff know who took the bag, and how did he get here before Mr. and Mrs. Dillon?"

"I think that woman can take care of herself, Patrick. Remarkable...," Maury shakes his head mulling what he had just heard. "I wouldn't want to be on her bad side, I'll tell ya that!"

Patrick finishes his drink and steps away from the bar. "I'd better get back. Kathleen needs me to keep her warm." Maury picks up his half empty glass, "Wait, I'll join ya." Patrick puts his hand on Maury's arm, "No, you stay here and finish your drink. I'll check on Christine and make sure she's alright."

Maury hesitates, then glances at Catherine making small talk with one of the men at the end of the bar, "Well, I'll be just a few more minutes."

"Atta boy, Maury!" Patrick slaps his back, "See ya in the morning! We start work on the trestle tomorrow."

Catherine sees Patrick's back as he exits and looks to see Maury now standing at the bar alone, his glass almost empty. Bottle in hand, she comes back to Maury, "One more, Mr. Murphy?"

"No, Ma'am. Thank you. Not tonight. You know… work in the morning."

"I respect a man who knows his limit, the meaning of which was unknown to my husband," she says.

"Uh, yes, your husband." Maury wanted an opening to raise the subject, and there it is. "Are you sure you can manage without him?"

Catherine leans in emphasizing her femininity and so close that Maury could smell a delicate perfume, sweet and fragrant waft up on the warm air from her blouse.

"Maury, Shamus was a defeated man when we left the homeland, and he never recovered. I tried my best for the two of us to make a go of it, but the more successful we were with this business, the more he drank until it got the better of him. I saw the anger in him building, and I was afraid he was going to hurt someone. He was certainly hurting himself, so I had to do something about it." Catherine's voice trails off as she wipes the bar in front of Maury.

"And what exactly did you do about it?"

Catherine looks straight into Maury's eyes, her face not more than six inches from his. She smiles, and with a twinkle in her eye she says, barely audible, "Let's just say circumstances were such that Mr. Dillon had the opportunity to make a bad decision. He's going to pay the price for his weakness, and the judge told me I am unlikely to ever see him again. After the sentencing, I petitioned the judge to declare our marriage dissolved, which he did, and now I can get on with my life." Maury is transfixed; eye to eye with this beautiful woman who was exuding optimism and command. He admires her spirit. He feels his heart pounding in his chest and blood rushing to his head. Catherine stands up straight and takes a swipe across the bar. Bringing her gaze back to Maury, "Yes, now I can get on with my life."

"Just what do you have in mind, Catherine?" asks Maury, curious as to what her answer would be, for surely this remarkable woman would have equally remarkable plans.

"I'm going to continue to do what I have been doing: follow the railroad up to Highgate and provide comfort for the workers and whoever passes by just as I do now." Catherine again leans in toward Maury. "Of course, there's plenty of work to do, and Christine's been a great help, but I may need to hire another worker before next season."

The sight and smell of Catherine's ample femininity, her gentle touch, and the sound of her soft voice awakens a part of Maury long buried and almost forgotten. So many thoughts are going through his mind all at once, he can't sort through them. Many years of struggle and effort just to survive had pushed his sexual desires deep inside, but now they are coming to the surface with a rush of desire.

"I… well…I'm sure you will do just fine, Mrs. Dillon…. Catherine," is all that would come out as he straightens up. He looks down the bar. Are others seeing what he is feeling? Could Catherine? Surely she knows what she is doing and knows she has Maury succumbing to her charms. Does she treat others this way? Is this just the way she does her business, or are her intentions directed to him alone? No answers are going to come tonight.

"Well, thank you for your hospitality, Catherine. I should go now," is all Maury could say. "Must I?" Maury asks himself. Yes. Yes. He has stayed too long. "Good night, Catherine." Maury turns for the door, and then stops, turns back around, and is about to say something more. Catherine smiles, and that stops him in his tracks. He touches the brim of his hat and turns once again for the door making his way back across the footbridge to his campsite. He tries his best to go right to sleep, but he can only think about the sight of Mrs. Dillon and the sweet aroma surrounding her.

Once in bed, the light from nearby fires flickers on the tent walls and dances on his eyelids, illuminating images of Catherine he couldn't suppress: her provocative poses just inches in front of him. His thoughts came one after another, "Could I resist her if we were ever alone? Should I? What, just what would it be like to press her up against the bar, lean in to kiss…. Dear Lord, I must go to sleep."

Chapter 19
ANOTHER PAYDAY COMES AND GOES

When I'm not taking care of business at the store, or in Jonesville tending to the supervisors' personal business, I make my rounds through the camps retrieving company property, noting any damaged tents or cookware, and generally keeping my eyes open and my deaf ears to the ground.

There's much talk about another payroll coming in today or tomorrow, but I know that Belknap is supposed to arrive with May's payroll today. In spite of the company missing most of the March and April payrolls, life in the camps goes on thanks to the company providing a food line and running accounts for the workers at the company store. But what else can the railroad do? It has to feed the crew. And what else can the workers do? They have to eat.

The workers, knowing payroll is due, are more animated than usual and their talk is peppered with anger about getting shorted last month and laced with cynicism about what to expect this month. I'm hearing the men making all kinds of threats if they don't get their full pay. But the company store is providing everything they need to get by, even if it means they are running up debts they may never be able to pay off. Another reason for their frustration may be that some of them have no money to patronize the tavern. But I am a gentleman's gentleman. Lucky gets table scraps, and I get enough wages to imbibe a wee bit from time to time.

That the men won't be happy, to me, is a foregone conclusion because I'm pretty sure they're not going to see their back pay, and they'll be lucky to get the full month's pay that's due. Just how they'll take the news is another matter.

Once the possibility of another missed payroll is raised, as naturally as night follows day, talk turns to what actions would be appropriate if their pay isn't forthcoming. Having been shorted pay last month, the men have no choice but to patronize the company store and become ever more indebted to the company, and the fact that the company is at the same time becoming more indebted to the workers is little consolation. Most of them had fled their native Ireland; the entire country having been legally looted by the conquering Brits. In this case the men's cynicism goes deeper than a missed payroll; it's founded on several hundred years of very bad experiences.

Truth be told, I'm a bit concerned myself having gone through just about all of last's month's wages. I find Lucky playing with some of the children, and I urge him to come with me back to the store where the managers are meeting and where the payroll is expected to be delivered. We walk in and see Barnum, Eggleston, and Barker leaning back, each in a chair, with their feet against a cold stove. I smile, nod, and set about keeping myself busy, and, as I do, Lucky looks at me appearing to expect some treat or to give him some reason why I urged him away from his playmates. Seeing no treat forthcoming, he finds a particular spot on the floor, circles it several times, and lays down. With his chin on an extended paw, he lets out a rather resigned sigh. See? That's exactly how ya get along here: Accept reality and find a comfortable place to sleep.

"Well, I'm worried," says Barker. "I heard from Bernie when he was delivering feed for the mules, that our account with them is a month behind, and that we wouldn't be getting any more deliveries unless the account is made current."

This is how it works: Cash payroll is put on a company train headed north out of Connecticut. As it stops along the way to pick up additional supplies and disgorge passengers, the suppliers demand their accounts be settled before they provide additional supplies. So, by the time the payroll reaches the construction site, it's been whittled down to almost nothing. I suspect that could be the case again this month.

What cash does make it to the site goes first to pay the supervisors, and whatever remains gets divided more or less evenly among the workers. At least that's what happened last year. This year the cash seems to be shorter. Belknap always sees that I get something, and, although it's not a full worker's share, I don't complain. I just smile and nod and count my blessings. Last month there was only enough left to pay a fraction of what was due the workers, even after what is owed to the company is taken into account. The actual amount of cash paid out to the few dozen workers with a positive balance was no more than pocket change. I heard some of the unmarried men say they hoped to take what they were owed and leave the site, but without money in their pockets they had no choice but to stay and hope for the best this month.

"I'm taking heart in the fact that Mr. Belknap left yesterday, and he's not back from Northfield yet which means he had a reason to wait overnight, and I bet that reason is the payroll," says Barnum, a jolly good fellow and always the optimist.

Small talk continues until the thud of boots on the porch announces Belknap's return. Belknap comes through the door, a small valise in hand, but he doesn't say anything until his hat and coat are off. "Gentlemen, there's very little leftover for payroll. The shareholders are short on their assessments, and I had to pay our suppliers. The Board bought the surrendered shares with IOU's, and our suppliers aren't taking our promises to pay anymore. So we're going to repeat last month's process. Set up a table inside here, and you three go out and give the same instructions to the men."

"Boss," says Barnum, "This could get ugly. The men are already wondering if they're ever going to see their pay, and there's some talk about them sitting down."

"We need to remind them we will continue to provide food and shelter and whatever they need as long as they continue to work. We'll tell them their accounts at the store will be paid by what they are owed. If anyone still complains, remind him that he will get nothing but trouble if he doesn't keep working. Debtors get thrown in jail."

"What about our pay?" asks Barker.

"We'll be getting three-fifth shares, and the company will sign for our rent at the hotel."

Hearing this, I'm thinking it might be best for me to be outside while payroll is handed out, or, rather, not handed out. Maybe that way I'll be associated with workers rather than with management should things turn ugly. And, this'll give me a better idea of just how the men are taking it. If there's going to be trouble, it's going to come from the workers rebelling against their treatment by the company, and the store might just be the easiest target of their frustration. So I give Lucky a nudge on my way to the door, and we both wander out as if we both had heard nothing.

Sometime later it turns out the workers aren't taking it well – not well at all. No sir! I see Mr. O'Reilly and Mr. Murphy off to one side in heated debate. O'Reilly has his finger rapidly poking at Mr. Murphy's chest. O'Reilly stops talkin' as I approach.

"Ah, he's OK, " says Mr. Murphy.

"I say, it ain't stealing if we take what they owe us. We've had three men killed in the woods already, leavin' two widows and a couple of orphans without any way to get by. They're not even payin' us the money they owe us, and, in my mind, they're stealing our labor, and that fucking sheriff is in their back pocket. And here we are," Patrick says as he spreads his arms to the sky; turning in a full circle, taking in the whole of the valley and surrounding woods. "Trapped in the middle of nowhere with no way out. We're no better than slaves, I tell ya." Patrick's words appear to carry weight with the other men within shouting distance.

"They're keeping a record of what they owe us, and we're getting fed," says Mr. Murphy. "The best thing for us is to continue to work, and settle up at the end of the season. Ya never know, maybe the company will have the money they owe us next month. In the meantime, we have a trestle to build."

"That's another thing," says Patrick. "Dear Christ! Did you hear how they're planning to build that damn thing? We're not going to be using milled timbers and bolts. No, sir, they expect the God damned thing to stay together using half logs and spikes. It'll shake apart the first time a train passes over."

Murphy doesn't defend the company's plan. He simply puts his hand on Patrick's shoulder and turns him toward their campsite. Two other fellas also in an animated discussion join them as they walk back in a light rain snaking their way among the tents, their feet sinking deep into the muddy earth.

This evening there are a number of fairly large congregations scattered around camp under a constant drizzle. I try the best I can to be inconspicuous, but I can't attain complete invisibility. Maybe because I'm not one of them, being a house monkey and all, the speech-making quiets down whenever I approach. Mixed with their curses aimed at the company are occasional references to the "fucking Brits" and stories of being beaten down by landlords and starved to death by a merciless black fungus. Not a good sign.

What I do learn is a growing number of the workers are getting angry enough to take some kind of action. They're frustrated and the pressure is building. Me? I'm going to stay out of the way. My heart's with the workers, but my room and board is in the hands of my keepers. Lucky and I both know who has the keys to the company's larder.

Chapter 20

HITTING FULL STRIDE

I'm up early the next day to help dish out porridge and biscuits for the workers. They're still grumbling about the constant rain and no payroll, but it's mixed with proud talk about the trestle. Despite continuing to feel the weight of the years of the oppression they had suffered under the iron boot of the Brits, oppression they thought they had escaped, they also feel a sense of pride in what they are accomplishing: extending the industrial arm of a new and burgeoning nation by laying track through the North Woods.

North American commerce is growing tentacles; spreading out in every direction from the population centers into the wilderness to harvest the raw materials that are so abundant and here for the taking; fueled by capital supplied by the rich and labor supplied by the famine. Civilization, Ho!

Within the big picture is the reality in which we live: the challenge of laying five miles of track through Northern Vermont and building a trestle to span the Onion River, pay or no pay. The river's still running high and fast with spring runoff bolstered by the constant rain. Good Christ, the rain won't stop! The ice is gone, but there's still frozen water locked in the ground on the north sides of the mountains, adding to the river's flow as the ground continues to thaw in the warming spring air.

By the time I finish serving the morning meal and help the cooks clean up, the trestle crew has most of the first bent assembled in the jig, and, dear Lord, it's a monstrosity! Using half-sawn logs instead of milled lumber for the uprights gives it the appearance of something inelegant and uncivilized. I decide to carry a bucket of water and a ladle among the workers, staying close to Stoughton as he inspects construction.

"You!" Stoughton points to a worker spiking a cross piece into a debarked log. "That log is not straight. Any bend or crook will be a point of weakness. Use only the straightest logs for the verticals. Replace that one," he says pointing to an outside timber. By this time, Barnum has joined us, and he's wearing a smile. Mr. O'Reilly is with him.

Stoughton turns to Barnum, "Why are you grinning?"

Barnum looks satisfied as his gaze goes from the woods and slowly swings around to the river, "Just nice to see us in full swing! The men have been onsite for a couple of months, and the crew in the woods," he gestures toward the back of the field, "are becoming good lumberjacks. The roughing crew is processing the logs as soon as they come out of the woods, and our stockpile of timber should keep your trestle crews busy. In the meantime, we're making the bed and laying ties on the far side, right on schedule."

Barnum looks back at Stoughton with a broader smile. "What's not to like?"

"Oh, and I want you to meet Mr. O'Reilly," Barnum says. "Mr. O'Reilly was a civil engineer back in the old country, and I thought he'd be useful assigned to the trestle crew."

Turning to Patrick, Barnum says, "Mr. O'Reilly, I'd like you to meet the company's engineer, Mr. Stoughton."

Patrick extends his hand, "How'd you do, Mr. Stoughton?"

Stoughton keeps his eyes on the work going on in front of him and slowly turns to reluctantly shake Patrick's hand. "I've done some road and bridge construction, but never built anything like this," says Patrick.

"Well, Mr. O'Reilly," Stoughton looks Patrick straight in the eye, "We just need you to help direct the efforts of the construction crews, and do whatever Mr. Eggleston and Mr. Barnum tell you to do. OK?"

"Yes, sir," Patrick says, "I can do that."

Stoughton turns back to Barnum, "It looks all well and good, but the trestle's going to be tricky, so we need to be vigilant about its construction." Stoughton lifts his hat and runs his fingers through his thinning hair. "I'm concerned about using spikes instead of bolts, so let's notch the uprights for the sills before we spike them into place."

"OK, but we do have the braces and bits from last season," says Barnum, "We could use them to bolt the sway braces to the uprights."

"We're not going to be bolting them this season. We'll be spiking them, too," says Stoughton.

"I'll have to let Eggleston know," replies Barnum.

Stoughton turns and does a double take when he sees me. He walks over to the first two bents in the jigs. I follow and hand out water to those who signal me. Meanwhile, Eggleston and Barnum start coaching the crews that are going to rope the bents downstream into position and the crew that is going to hoist the bents into place. Patrick stays close to them, listening to every word.

Patrick walks over to the area where the first bent is nearing completion, and comes sprinting back to Barnum.

"Sir? It would be helpful if we had some buckets so we can keep the banks soaking wet. That'll make it easier for the bents to slide into the river. What do you think?"

Barnum appears pleasantly surprised, "The banks are plenty wet from the rain, but that's a good idea. Go get two buckets from the tool shed, and tell Mickey I said it's OK." Patrick returns with the buckets and directs the ropers to wet the bank as needed.

Everyone within sight of the project stops his work as the first bent is lifted from its jig. Accompanied by a lot of shouting and gestures, it's eased into the rushing water tethered by four ropes held by eight men. As it floats into place, sharpened feet first, the two men with ropes tied to the far side of the bent pull hard, lifting the far side out of the water, sinking the near side into the river bottom. The bent stands straight up in the water. Two planks are dropped onto the cap; a man scrambles up each one and spikes them into the cap while two others spike the ends of the planks into the stakes sticking out of the granite approach on shore. A collective cheer and applause rises up from everyone within sight as it is secured in place; a milestone reached.

By the end of the first day of trestle construction three double bents are up, and the first five men are starting to spike the stringers across the tops, tying the bents together. Work is slow and precarious. Ropes tether the men to the bents, and workers get tangled in the structure while moving among the timbers. The footing on the slick structure is unsure while below the still icy Onion rushes by, waiting to grab an errant foot and drag the owner under.

I make myself useful all day. When I'm not helping with the day's meals, I'm running among the trestle crew with water and tending to minor injuries. A certain pride is spreading throughout the camp. The worksite is in full song. Grumbling about the short payroll has subsided, replaced by the growing satisfaction of each man becoming more skilled at his job; each crew becoming more skilled in executing their part of the process: crew handing off material to the next crew, and then onto the next; and finally seeing the trestle starting to take shape.

The next few days are productive. The crews struggled to get started, and after getting a good sense of their place in the project, there are fewer accidents and daily progress is increasing. Everyone seems to have hit full stride. A symphony of sound fills the valley as the season finds its rhythm. The trestle is our opera, currently in dress rehearsal – the staccato percussion of the axe against timber, the rhythm of a pit saw ripping its way through a log, accompanying the arias of men in full voice. A symphony of construction conducted by a quintet of supervisors.

Chapter 21

COW'S MILK FOR THE CALVES

With the trestle taking shape a sense of celebration is in the air, and more men than usual are at Catherine's tonight. The tavern was closed last Sunday while Catherine took the buckboard west and north to restock, returning a few days later with crates of Canadian liquor. Either she's found a way to elude the law at the border, or she's paid the right people to look the other way. Whatever the case, she knows her business.

By the time my chores are done and I make my way to the tavern there's standing room only. It's so busy Catherine enlisted the help of Mr. Strong, the blacksmith from Jonesville, putting him to work behind the bar pouring drinks from the shelves of bottles, flasks, and decanters while Catherine works the floor. I'm surprised to see Sheriff Ferris here, too, at a table in the far corner with Belknap and Barnum. Knots of men are standing in groups of three and four, shoulder to shoulder, and the doors are wide open to let in the spring night air and to let out the smoke of Carolina cigars Catherine has for sale. Mr. Murphy, O'Reilly, and Noonan are near the end of the bar.

Catherine must have anticipated a busy night. There's a wide variety of drink available along with shards of jerky, salted cod and haddock, and biscuits. In addition to the distilled liquors Catherine brought in from Canada, men are ordering Brandy, Holland Gin, and a liquor that's called New England rum, a drink distilled from molasses. Keeping in mind the uncertainty of future paydays, I favor the less expensive hard apple cider.

When I was down in Connecticut over the winter, the temperance movement was in full swing with heated debates taking place in taverns as well as on town commons and in church. But, ha! The voices of temperance are too far away to be heard at Catherine's! Given the nature of our makeshift town here on Bolton Flats, a plea for temperance would not be well received.

Nights like this one are great fun. Hardly noticed as I wander about the room, I am able to listen in on any conversation. No matter what I hear I just turn my head this way and that, smiling and nodding like an idiot, and every once in awhile someone buys the smiling deaf guy a drink. Making my way from the bar with my cider I stand with my back to Mr. O'Reilly and hear him talking to Mr. Murphy about his concerns with the trestle construction. He's excited to see it coming together, but thinks using un-milled timbers and spikes at all the joints is not a good idea.

Catherine is working the room wearing trousers and boots, an apron, and a blouse that's provocatively unbuttoned. Around her neck hangs a gold chain with a cross dangling in the deep recess of her bosom. She makes her way gracefully from the bar to one table and then the next and back again, all the while laughing and joking with her customers she calls by name. The place is packed, but it seems to me she goes a bit out of her way on each return trip to the bar to squeeze between Mr. Murphy and O'Reilly, always facing Mr. Murphy, and Patrick notices. I can see as she passes she looks directly into Murphy's eyes and smiles. She doesn't smile at anyone else that way.

"Damn, Maury, she is one fancy woman, and she seems to like you," says Patrick.

"I haven't been with a woman since my Elizabeth passed, but Catherine has me thinking some very sinful thoughts!" Maury let out a laugh and sips his drink.

"Well, I'm married, and I'm also thinking some sinful thoughts, my friend," says Patrick.

Catherine delivers her drinks to the table where Sheriff Ferris sits, his menacing gaze follows her as she makes her way back to the bar. As she passes, men shout out for refills, and Catherine remembers each one.

Again, she chooses a path that takes her by Mr. Murphy, and she stops to talk. I hear her comment about the work Mr. Murphy's daughter will be doing the next day, but apparently Ferris dislikes what he is seeing and gets up from his chair. He staggers as he makes his way through the crowd, keeping his balance by bumping against other patrons, unaware he caused several drinks to slosh over their brims.

Ferris, clearly under the influence of his drink, approaches Mr. Murphy, "What's your interest in Mrs. Dillon, Mick?" Not waiting for an answer, he continues, poking his finger in Maury's chest, "I don't like you, and I don't like you talking with her. Understand?"

Maury pushes his hand away, "I don't see how that is any of your business, Sheriff."

"Anything that goes on in my territory is my business, Mick, so watch what you do." Ferris looks into his tankard and takes a swig, some of which trickles into his unkempt beard.

"Let me ask you something, Sheriff," says Maury. "Where're you from?"

"That's none of your fucking business, Mick, but if you must know I come from Kilkenny. And have no doubt, I got here long before you, and I'm going to be here long after you're gone. I'm the law here, and I'm tellin' you to stay away from Mrs. Dillon."

Maury persists, "What was your profession back home, Sheriff?"

"That's none of your God damned business either, Mick." Ferris squints unfocused up into Maury's face, then turns and staggers back to his table.

"What was that all about?" asks Patrick.

"He's just drunk," says Maury, "but he's just as nasty sober, I'll tell ya! I just want to understand what makes him so belligerent toward his fellow countrymen. He says he's from Kilkenny, but I'm not familiar with any family from there named 'Ferris'." Maury pauses, takes a drink, and adds, "He scares Christine half to death."

Patrick, glancing back at Ferris says, "I don't like that son of a bitch."

After a moment of silence they look at each other and then look down at me! It's all I can do to just smile, and act like I didn't hear what they had just said. So I motion over toward Ferris, then scowl and shake my head. Unable to participate in the conversation, I take another drink and turn away. I know Ferris to be an ornery bastard, and I've seen him look at Catherine with an evil eye. So now that Shamus is gone, I have concerns about Catherine's safety, but she's certainly safe in the company of her customers tonight.

Every now and then a small group of men breaks into song, like a sweet breeze floating over the din of the room, and those around them cease their talk and listen. Wilbur is here with his pipe, and one of the workers has a fiddle. As spirits continue to flow, an ode to whiskey moves everyone to sing with the chorus, "bainne na mbó do na gamhna", meaning "…cow's milk for the calves":

In the sweet county Lim'rick, one cold winter's night
All the turf fires were burning when I first saw the light;
And a drunken old midwife went tipsy with joy,
As she danced round the floor with her slip of a boy,
Singing bainne na mbó do na gamhna
And the juice of the barley for me!

Then when I was a young lad of six years or so,
With me book and my pencil to school I did go,
To a dirty old school house without any door,
Where lay the school master blind drunk on the floor,

Singing bainne na mbó do na gamhna
And the juice of the barley for me!

At the learning I wasn't such a genius I'm thinking,
But I soon beat the master entirely at drinking,
Not a wake or a wedding for five miles around,
But meself in the corner was sure to be found.

Singing bainne na mbó do na gamhna
And the juice of the barley for me!
Then one Sunday the priest read me out from the altar,

Saying you'll end your days with your neck in a halter;
And you'll dance a fine jig betwix heaven and hell,
And his words they did haunt me the truth for to tell,

Singing bainne na mbó do na gamhna
And the juice of the barley for me!

So the very next morn as the dawn it did break,
I went down to the priest house the pledge for to take,
And in there in the room sat the priests in a bunch,
Round a big roaring fire drinking tumblers of punch,

Singing bainne na mbó do na gamhna
And the juice of the barley for me!

Well from that day to this I have wandered alone,
I'm a jack of all trades and a master of none,
With the sky for me roof and the earth for me floor,
And I'll dance out my days drinking whiskey galore,

Singing bainne na mbó do na gamhna
And the juice of the barley for me!

Aye! The joy of good fellowship warmed with the juice of the barley. By the final chorus, all have joined in, and a cheer punctuates the final note. Then, without missing a beat, someone starts singing a song that laments lost love – love for another and love for country: "The Girl I Left Behind Me." As the first words left the lips of one man, all join in, and the place is in solemn chorus with cups reverently held high.

All the dames of France are fond and free
And Flemish lips are really willing.
Very soft the maids of Italy
And Spanish eyes are so thrilling.
Still, although I bask beneath their smile,

Their charms will fail to bind me,
And my heart falls back to Erin's isle
To the girl I left behind me.

Silence. Not a sound is heard for time enough for each man to recall memories of loved ones and the beloved homeland left behind. More than one sleeve is lifted to wipe away a tear. It is some comfort that this valley surrounded by lush green mountains and laced with streams of clear water is reminiscent of her majesty, Lady Ireland.

Chapter 22

CLOSING TIME

I spend the rest of the evening wandering around the room, standing here and there, often hearing about friends and family and the hardships suffered back home. Many of us have similar stories: family farms divided into smaller and smaller plots, generation after generation, as a result of the inheritance laws, having no choice but to become tenant farmers and sharecroppers. A nice arrangement… if you're British, that is!!

Over time, the entire country was legally enslaved by Parliamentary legislation authored and adopted by the enslavers. Quite a game!! And you can always win a game if you're the one making up the rules. What's legal and what's moral often have two different answers.

After attending the board meeting, I could see the same happening with our current endeavor. Everyone hears about the money to be made by investing in railroad stock, but what isn't widely known is stockholders have to surrender their shares if they don't have the cash when the company's board decides to assess each shareholder additional cash to keep operating. Everyone's playin' by the rules, but it appears the more management mismanages the business, the richer they become. That, too, is quite a game! And so it goes.

Passing the evening in Catherine's tavern has been a great pleasure. Men are feeling the effects of Catherine's spirits on top of the satisfaction of getting a foothold in the New World. Toward the end of the evening I see Barnum help the sheriff make his way to his horse, hoist him up onto the steed, point him toward Jonesville, and swat the critter's behind. The tavern empties steadily, and blacksmith Strong departs after finishing his duties. Mr. Murphy and Mr. O'Reilly take an empty table while I remain at the bar and nurse my last few sips. It's getting late, and eventually, Mr. O'Reilly returns to camp leaving only Mr. Murphy and me behind. I sit down at a table in the far corner with my gaze fixed on the open door across the room. Catherine pulls a chair up next to Mr. Murphy.

"This was one hell of a night, don't you think?" says Catherine. "I love nights like this." She takes a small white lace cloth from her apron pocket and dabs at her face. While looking directly at Murphy, she wipes her neck, and slowly pushes aside her blouse as she pats at the moisture glistening on her pale skin. "Would you like another drink, Maury?"

"No, I...no thank you, Catherine." He looks up having followed the movement of her hand. Holding up his glass, "I've been working on this last one slowly so I can work tomorrow, but I'm finding it difficult to leave. I thought I can stay as long as I have something in my glass," he says, smiling.

Resting my head on my arms crossed on the table, I turn just enough to enable me to see that Catherine has situated herself with one leg across Murphy's leg under the table. I don't want to be caught staring, but this is one conversation I want to hear, so I turn my head away from where they sit. Oh, what a great time to be invisible! Maybe they will ignore the deaf and dumb house monkey.

"You don't need an excuse to be here, Maury," Catherine says in a soft whisper.

The momentary silence is broken by the sound of a chair moving across the rough floorboards, and then I feel a hand on my shoulder. Damn! Looking up, Catherine has a smile on her face and a hand under my arm. She motions me toward the door. Reluctantly, I get up and tip my hat to both as I walk out the door and feel the cool night air against my reddened face. The evening's drizzle has ended, and the sky is star-lit. I linger outside the tavern just long enough to see Catherine walk back toward where Mr. Murphy is sitting. He pulls the chair out for her to sit, but, instead, she moves the chair away from the table and slowly lifts one leg over his lap and sits with her hands clasped around his neck. Without hesitating, Maury moves one hand to the small of her back, the other curls around the nape of her neck, and he pulls her lips toward his.

Yes, yes, I want to stay and watch what would follow, but I'm a decent man, mostly, and I still have some sense of right and wrong. So I head back through the moonlit night, over the footbridge to camp. Once across the river I turn and see that all but one of the tavern lights has been extinguished.

The night is perfectly still, and the constant chirp of crickets drown out any other sound. The thought of companionship moves me to find Lucky asleep outside the store, and I bring him inside to sleep near my cot.

I don't know how or when Mr. Murphy's night ended, but mine ends with my imagination fully engaged, yet quickly succumbing to a sleep induced by hard cider.

Chapter 23

TROUBLED WATERS

Several hours before sunrise, booming storms roll through the valley, west to east, releasing sheets of wind-blown rain accompanied by deafening thunder that caroms off the steep mountain walls enclosing the flats. A brief period of high winds brings down more than a few tents, and we hear trees cracking in the woods.

There's much talk about it raining as much here as back in Ireland. What the new workers don't know is this year's rain has been heavier and much more frequent than last year's. Making conditions worse, there's a lot of clay in the soil, so the ground stays wet longer, giving way under boot and clinging to hand and foot. The deep, muddy ground around the tents hasn't dried out since our arrival and it frequently sucks the boots off a man mid-stride. At first, the sight of man whose raised foot is unexpectedly bootless was humorous, but now it's just another irritant along with the constant swarms of black flies and mosquitoes. Many men now leave their tents bare foot, carrying boots and liners directly to the river where they wash the mud off their feet, and only then do they put their boots on.

This morning's downpour has freshened the air, and it's a pleasure to take that first full breath in the morning. Spring is warming into summer, and the bird songs are becoming a louder and more constant presence. Spirits are high from yesterday's progress on the trestle even among those of us who had spent entirely too much time at Catherine's. As work crews gather, Foreman Eggleston approaches each group of men working on the trestle with the same caution, "Last night's rain is going to bring the river up later today and tomorrow, so keep tools and materials well back from the bank. The current will quicken, too, so I'll bring over extra help for the crews floating the bents into place."

No tellin' how much rain fell throughout the region last night. Could've been an isolated line that quickly passed overhead, or a drenching of the whole watershed that will take awhile to make its way into the streams and tributaries coming down the mountains into the already swift flowing Onion. The river is still cold, and the current is swollen from the constant rain making its way into the river.

The bents already in place are wet and slippery, but now, with some experience, the men working in the trestle's structure are getting their footing and feeling more comfortable with their tasks. As a precaution, the men working in the trestle tie themselves to the structure at the end of rope tethers to prevent falling into the river in case they lose their footing.

The spirit and pace of work is gaining momentum encouraged by the birdsong, the percussion of axe and sledge, and the rhythmic rush of the river. Our North Woods opera is in full voice.

In spite of the heavy overnight downpour and lingering drizzle, progress continues throughout the day and into the next. The river continues to rise and the pace of its flow is increasing, yet the bents already erected, though not yet connected to the far side, stand firm in place.

I heard Barnum say he was told by the driver who brought supplies to the camp that all of the North Woods got drenched with the recent rain, enough to flood low-lying areas, but not enough to affect our work. That report was passed along to the other supervisors, and the crew working in the trestle were reminded to use their tethers.

The river's flotsam includes occasional tree branches of various sizes, some dead, some leafed out, and all rushing by on the rolling current. It's midday, and work has hit full stride. A routine has set in: piecing together the bents on shore; dragging each one to the river to be tied to leads and sliding it into the rushing current; guided into place to be secured to the bents already erected. Once in place, each double bent requires four stringers, two sills, and additional sway braces before the next bent can be sited. We're nearly halfway across, so there are more than a twenty men working in the partially completed structure.

Thanks to the heavy rains and rising water, additional hands are needed to guide the completed bents into place and resist being swept away by the increasingly swift and powerful current. So I'm recruited to join a crew and take a rope. I'd forgotten how powerful the turbulent water can be. Each floating bent tugs on the ropes and tries to drag every man into the torrent of water and debris. I keep my deaf head down and concentrate on maintaining my footing on the wet clay and grass made slick by the constant rain and make every effort not to respond to the shouts and cautions of my co-workers.

With more hands than usual on the ropes and a multitude of voices barking orders, it takes me awhile to discern the frantic message of several men upstream shouting, "Hey! Watch out! Watch out!"

Spontaneously, I turn my head right along with everyone else and see that the next bent to be floated down river has slid into the river un-tethered and is careening toward the half-completed trestle that now looks like a fragile house of cards.

"Get down from there! Get down," shouts a panicked Eggleston pointing upstream. Several of the men laying the stringers on top scamper toward shore and jump to safety. Others working among the bents, in their surprise, lose their footing and fall into the substructure, saved temporarily by their tethers. Others, un-tethered, fall directly into the water and are swept toward the footbridge by the swift current. The men working in the substructure and tethered to it, can see their fates are tied to that of the trestle. As the errant bent draws closer, the men in the structure are pulling frantically at their tethers, trying to untie them, their heads turning rapidly from their ropes to the oncoming mass of timber bearing down on them and back to the ropes imprisoning them.

The free-floating bent catches the outermost three bents, jarring the entire construct, pushing two bents over, ripping them from the structure and dislodging two more. There are six men still tied to the bents floating down river. Three of the men who had been working on top fall into the river and flail about in the ice-cold water. The current pushes one free-floating man toward shore where he is pulled out, but the other two are unable to keep their heads above water and are swept under the footbridge and down river.

The commotion has drawn the attention of those on shore, including Patrick, who throws a line toward the tangle of men and timber. One man, tied to a bent, manages to grab the rope, and even with half a dozen hands trying to pull him in, the weight of the bent and the force of the river pull the rope along with some flesh from their hands; the river taking control once again.

Others run to the footbridge and drop lines into the water for men to grab as they pass under. One of the bents, askew in the water, is lodged against the footbridge with one man clinging to the timber, his head above water. Hands reach down and pull him up. The bodies of two others tied to the bent pass under the bridge. One, still tethered to a timber, pops out from under the bridge, but his body is being twisted and dunked in the fast current. The other man is trapped under the bridge, and either a timber or the man's skull is repeatedly banging against the underside of the deck.

Some of the women and children moving toward the scene are stopped and told to stay back, a directive most ignore. They could see what has happened, and those whose husbands are working in the trestle are frantic, adding to the turmoil.

In just a few minutes the "incident," as management later referred to it, is over. Four men had jumped to safety, one swam to shore, and one with a broken arm was pulled from the tangle of timber and debris lodged in the footbridge. Eggleston did a head count and concluded, in all, six men were lost, and two crippled: the man with a broken arm and another with a broken leg from his jump to safety.

I know from past experience the gentlemen with the broken limbs will be told to pack up their belongings, settle their accounts at the company's store, and leave camp. They're no longer of any use to the railroad.

Lifeless at the end of their tethers, one body tied to the bent lodged under the footbridge was solemnly retrieved while the two other tethered bodies downstream from the footbridge bob in the water like kites in a strong wind. About an hour later a soaked and trembling man bleeding from his scalp had somehow managed to save himself and was walking up the Stage Road toward camp. His wife, with two little ones trailing, is the first to reach him, and others help him to the aid station set up in front of the store. In spite of Barker and Eggleston directing men to return to work, the work around camp stops while the injured are cared for and the families of the dead are consoled.

Chapter 24

PLAN B

Emotions are running high fueled by adrenalin, the loss of life, and by the seriousness of the tasks at hand. Little direction is been needed for the workers and wives providing care for the injured and consolation to the families of the victims, while others appear to be running here and there without direction or purpose.

Mr. Murphy stopped his work when the commotion began and eventually found Patrick in a heated discussion with Mr. Eggleston. "If the stringers and braces were bolted instead of spiked, they've held against the current," insists Patrick, angry and moving to stay in front of Eggleston as he tries to turn away. "Ya shouldn't be using un-milled timber for the bents. Ya gotta have a better joint to take a bolt. Those spikes just pulled right out!"

Eggleston, unable to escape Patrick, turns and stands his ground. "Look, Pat, our engineer said the design and materials are adequate, and the board of directors approved. So that's the end of the discussion."

Patrick has no retort, so Eggleston goes over to what remains of the trestle and joins Freeman and Belknap who are directing the salvage effort.

Maury catches up to Patrick, "Patrick!"

Still enraged, Patrick turns toward the voice calling his name. "I questioned using the God-damned un-milled timbers when I first saw 'em," says Patrick as if Maury had been a part of the preceding conversation, "and it looks like nothing's going to change. Damn it! It ain't safe. It ain't safe, and now we have more dead to bury. We're just takin' the railroad's God damned soup."

"Maybe when they have time to take a look at what happened and think about it, they'll listen to ya," offers Maury. He puts his arm around Patrick's shoulder, "'Till then, let's see what we can do to help."

Belknap, Barker, Barnum, Freeman, Eggleston, and I are weaving through the pockets of men, women, and children congregated near the riverbank. "Go back to your jobs, gentlemen," they repeat. Freeman is the closest to Patrick, and overhears him talking to Maury. "The excitement's over, and we're taking care of business, Mr. O'Reilly," he says. Just as Patrick is about to share his thoughts with supervisor Freeman, Maury grabs Patrick's arm and pulls him back. "Not now, Patrick." Patrick pauses, and Maury says, "I'll see you at the end of the day. We'll go to Catherine's later."

I watch as Mr. Murphy and O'Reilly disappear into the sea of men heading back into the camp. I find Barker, Belknap, and Barnum heading back to the store, and I follow three paces behind. I can't quite make out their conversation because there is still quite a bit of shouting and grieving, and as we reach the store, Barnum turns to see Lucky and me in his wake. This is no time for tail wagging, and both Lucky and I know it. We keep our heads down and stay a respectful distance behind. There are several men and a few women at the store wanting to get in, and as Barnum opens the door, they anxiously push in asking for supplies to treat the injured.

Says Belknap to Barnum, "See what they want." And pointing to me, "Have Doug keep track of who's taken what, and don't give away the store."

Barnum motions for me to stand at the counter. He places a piece of paper in front of me, brings up a quill and a tin of ink from under the counter, and writes "Name" and "Item" at the top with a line drawn top to bottom dividing the two words and forming two columns. I nod and take up the quill.

I stand at the counter while Barker and Belknap speak quietly near the back. Two men take a paper bag of salt (20 ounces), a yard of cheesecloth, and two balls of twine; then rush out. I close the door behind them so I can hear Barker and Belknap and busy myself restocking and cleaning up.

"I had my doubts using un-milled logs for the bents, and now I have my answer," says Belknap. "Let's talk with Stoughton. Maybe we can get his support to go back to using milled timbers and bolts. That trestle would've held if it was bolted, and we just lost two or more weeks' work to clean-up and rebuild."

"So what do you want us to tell the men?" asks Barker.

"Just go find Stoughton, and tell him to come see me," directs Belknap. Barker heads out. There are quite a few folks congregated outside the store, and I can hear several say they want to come in to talk with Belknap, but Barker says Belknap is busy, and closes the door, keeping them out.

Belknap stomps his foot to get my attention, then points to the floor and makes a sweeping motion. I get a broom and start cleaning up, and a few minutes later Mr. Stoughton bursts into the store, pale and stunned, as if he had just seen a ghost.

"Several of the people outside want to talk to you, George," says Stoughton addressing Belknap, "and they seem a bit heated."

Stoughton makes his way to the rear of the store where Belknap is sitting. He does a double take when he sees me at work.

"George, I think we can make the rough timber design work if we bind the spiked joints with rope. What do ya think? I mean, Rake's not going to want to go back to using milled timbers. Do you think he'd change his mind and go back to using milled timbers and bolts?"

"You're the engineer, Phillip," says Belknap. "I'm looking to you to tell us how to proceed. Do we re-build and continue with the current design, or go back to the proven method of using milled timbers and bolts?"

"Well, let's see… it would take us at least two days to get the bolts and the extra braces and drill bits we'd need if we revert to the old method. But Mr. Rake is convinced the new design is worth the risk, and I'm not going to argue with Mr. Rake. No sir!"

Stoughton never did impress me as a man who would stand up to Paine or Rake, right or wrong. I don't think this is going to turn out well. After a pause, apparently thinking about it, Belknap says, "Listen. Let's re-build what's left of the trestle with your idea to tie the spiked joints.

That'll take several days and give you time to go and tell Rake or Paine what has happened. You can tell them I recommend going back to the old design so we don't suffer any more setbacks. I'll brief Eggleston and Freeman on the plan, and get the men started re-building. We have a supply car coming up at first light tomorrow, and you can head back south when it leaves."

Appearing relieved, Stoughton says, "Alright. Yes, yes, I can do that. So, I can tell Mr. Rake we started rebuilding right away, and see what he says about finishing the trestle." Stoughton rises and heads to the door, turning back over his shoulder to Belknap, "Yes, I'll talk to Mr. Rake, and let him know we started rebuilding." Stoughton is brought up short when he opens the door and finds a knot of workers outside facing him. He steps back in and closes the door.

Belknap looks at Stoughton, "You can tell Rake I recommend using the old method of milled timbers and bolts, and tell Freeman and Eggleston to plan on going to Catherine's tonight. At least one of us should be over there every night to keep an eye on what's happening among the men. I don't want this situation to get out of hand. And tell Freemen and Eggleston about tying the spiked joints and to pass the word among the crews. That should ease the men's concern about our rebuild."

Stoughton nods and pauses as his hand goes back to the door's latch. He quickly opens it and walks out. Through the open door I can see Mr. O'Reilly approach him, so I continue my sweeping out on the porch.

O'Reilly doesn't hold back, "Who's idea was it to use un-milled timber and spikes in the assembly? Who thought that was going to work?" Not waiting for an answer, Mr. O'Reilly continues, "The whole God damned thing should be taken down and done correctly. The next heavy rain could undo whatever we get done, and we'll have wasted more time and more lives."

I can see Stoughton wants to respond, but seems just as happy to let Patrick continue his rant. "Christ, man! Ya just lost all the time you saved by takin' your shortcuts, and ya took the lives of some good men along with it."

The truth of Patrick's last comment seemed to stab at Stoughton's conscience. "Sir, our design was approved by a structural engineer," failing to say he is that structural engineer. "And the company's Board of Directors approved it."

Seeing that he has to say something conciliatory, Stoughton starts to walk away saying to anyone listening and waving his hand over his head in a dismissive manner, "We're going to rebuild with an improved design. It'll make the joints more secure." Stoughton pushes through the small crowd, and heads toward the broken trestle.

As Patrick starts to walk off several other men join him. I hear one say, "I'm not going to work another day until they change the way we build that damn thing. It's a death trap."

This is beginning to feel familiar. In the old country, constantly living under the boot of injustice, good souls, born subtle and accepting, are hardened after acquiring emotional scar tissue, becoming inflexible and less sensitive. Back home, talk of resentment, resistance, and revolution began in taverns and meeting halls, so I'm not going to miss tonight's gathering at Catherine's.

Chapter 25

CONSTRUCTION RESUMES

The rhythm found after days of productivity has been lost to the unanticipated, unwelcome, and destructive intrusion of nature. With the dark cloud of lives lost hanging over the valley, gloom and anger has replaced pride and optimism. The next day those who return to work spend as much time talking as they do working, and given the general mood, the supervisors don't crack their whips as they normally would. Maybe a dozen men, without asking permission, take on the tasks of caring for the bodies of the dead, consoling their families, and making preparations for burials. Another small group attend to the injured, and skilled hands set about making several pairs of crutches. I hear Belknap instruct Barker to record the names of the men not doing the railroad's work so they can be docked their day's pay.

Their day's pay? Ha! Most haven't seen a full day's pay since they started workin'.

The errant bent is still wedged under the footbridge, so a crew is assembled to retrieve the pieces of broken trestle. The bents furthest from the shore had yielded to the force of the run-away timber propelled by the flood currents, while several other bents, still held by the stringers are askew and just need to be pulled upright and reseated on the river bed. Two weeks' work undone will be a three week setback.

These early June days are getting longer, so even after the evening meal those who haven't headed to Catherine's mill about in small groups scattered among the tents. Standing on the store porch I can see Mr. Murphy walking among the tents perhaps looking for Mr. O'Reilly who is holding court with a group of men all very animated in their manner as Mr. Murphy draws closer. I also can see Barnum walking among the tents and approaching O'Reilly's group.

I can't hear a word from where I'm standing, but a gentleman's gentleman should be handy in case his master needs him, true? So I hurry through the maze of tents, but slow down as I approach trying to appear as if I just happened upon the scene.

Jabbing a finger at Barnum's chest, Mr. O'Reilly's eyes are ablaze, "How many of us said the spikes wouldn't hold? How many of us told you using un-milled timbers made for poor joints? God damn it, man! Now you have deaths on your hands."

"Our engineer has a fix for the spiked joints," Barnum replies, not taking O'Reilly's bait.

Other voices want to be heard, but Barnum raises his hands. "Hold on, hold on! We're going to rebuild the trestle using a better way of securing the joints. We don't want more setbacks anymore than you do."

Patrick is livid, "Setbacks? Setbacks? Is that what you call this murderous calamity? A setback? Well, fuck you!"

"You watch your tone, O'Reilly. You...all of you, can be replaced. We have a job to do and we're going to do it. Accidents happen." With that said, Barnum turns and disappears into the fading light of day.

"Patrick!" Mr. Murphy catches up with his friend, "Jesus, man, be careful what you say to the bosses or you'll find yourself out on your ass," he says grabbing Mr. O'Reilly's arm. "Come on. Go tell Kathleen I'm taking you over to Catherine's to cool down."

I catch O'Reilly's eye, and he starts to say something to me, but catches himself. He doesn't look like a man who wants to cool down or who is able to cool down. Thinking it's best for me to disappear, I return to the store and find Belknap talking to Barnum and Eggleston. When I open the door the serious expressions on their faces turn to surprise, perhaps expecting a lynch mob. Clearly irritated that it is I who startled them, I pretend to look for something behind the counter and leave just as quickly as I had appeared. All I heard in the few moments I was there was this from Barnum, "If we don't build it right it'll be a death trap."

Outside once again, I realize I don't belong here - not a member of management, and not accepted as a member of the crew. Don't the men realize when all is said and done I am one of them? Is it time for my hearing to return? If so, I may end up working in the scaffolding of the trestle and find myself lodged under the footbridge bobbing at the end of a rope. Nope, I'm safer being a house monkey for the rest of the season. At least I can keep the company of Lucky and the patrons at Catherine's.

Chapter 26

BURY THE DEAD

Mr. Murphy and O'Reilly make their way to Catherine's door moments before I do. Inside, instead of the usual loud din of gentlemen at leisure, the room is full of hushed conversation among groups of men leaning in toward one another and looking side to side. Several are standing at the bar, and even Catherine appears subdued. She wipes her hands on her apron as she walks toward her two new customers.

"The accident today was such a tragedy," she says, putting her hand on Mr. Murphy's arm and giving O'Reilly a sympathetic look. "Christine and I didn't get a chance to talk today, Maury. How is she doing?"

"Christine has seen her share of suffering. Perhaps she thought she had seen the last of it because this tragedy has her quite upset," he replies. "Of course, she's also worried about my well being, but I assured her my work doesn't come with the same dangers as the men on the trestle."

After a moment of thought, Catherine says, "Why don't you ask Christine if she'd like to stay with me for awhile? Things will be quiet here for the next few days, and she's here everyday anyway. You'll be right across the river, and you could even come and tuck her in at night." Catherine's hand is still resting on Maury's arm, "We girls would both like that."

Mr. Murphy keeps his gaze on Catherine, but doesn't answer. I see him swallow hard and wonder if he would ever be able to say another word! "Well...I...I'll ask Christine. I'm sure she'd like that, Catherine. Thank you. That's very nice of you."

"Come in and sit down. I'll set you up," she says. Catherine turns toward the bar and, glancing in my direction, she gives me a wink. The two men find a table at the far end of the room, and I decide to stand at the bar near their table. They order rums and Catherine pours my usual hard cider.

Almost in a whisper Patrick says, "I tell ya, Maury, we have to do something. What happened today could happen again. They have us stuck out here in the middle of nowhere, they haven't paid us, and now they've killed five more men."

"You heard the engineer, they're going to take steps to secure the joints. It doesn't make sense for them to risk losing weeks' more work," Maury replies. "And, I don't see an alternative."

O'Reilly continues, "I've talked to two dozen men, and without an exception they all agreed: The answer is for us all to refuse to work until the trestle is built properly and we get paid the money they owe us." His fist hits the table hard, and heads turn toward him.

I felt the force of O'Reilly's frustration through the floorboards. So could everyone else in the room. Freeman and Eggleston are sitting two tables away, and I don't think they heard his words, but everyone could see the anger in Mr. O'Reilly's face. Mr. Murphy leans in close to him, "Patrick, you should be careful what you say. It's better to have the choice to stay and to work or not. Having your own choice is better than having the choice made for you. If they think you're going to cause trouble, you won't have a choice. You'll be fired and thrown out of the camp. Having choices is real wealth, my friend."

Turning back toward the bar, I don't hear either of them say anything for quite a few minutes. Getting up from their table, Mr. Murphy and O'Reilly head toward the door, and while Mr. Murphy stops to say something to Catherine, Mr. O'Reilly stops at several tables and whispers something to the workers at each one.

A few minutes after O'Reilly and Mr. Murphy depart, several other tables of workers get up and leave the tavern half empty and eerily quiet. Standing alone at the bar, I have just a bit of cider left to down, so I wander toward Eggleston and Freeman. As I approach, they stand, finish what's left in their tankards, and bid Catherine good night.

Good night? The sun had not been down more than an hour, and the last of Catherine's patrons are out the door, leaving me alone with her. I reach into my pouch for a coin to leave on the bar when Catherine walks over and stands between me and the exit. The woman is as tall as I, and she stands straight up, wiping her hands.

Looking directly into my eyes she says, "The men are very upset, Doug. What is the company going to do about rebuilding the trestle?"

I freeze in my tracks. She knows I'm deaf. I've pulled off my charade successfully for almost a year, and had done a damn good job at it, too. Moreover, I hadn't said any more than a garbled word or two to anyone for about as long. The only sounds I uttered this past year were occasionally singing an Irish tune poorly and talking out loud to myself to add to the oddness of the character I had adopted. Now I have this woman asking me a question as if I can hear her and as if I can give her an answer? Had I slipped up somehow?

"Doug, I've seen you lean in to hear conversations you weren't supposed to hear. I don't think anyone else suspects, but I'm thinkin' you can hear just fine. Your secret's safe with me. I just want to know what's going on in the camps." Catherine stands her ground. "I'll make a bargain with you: For every bit of important information you bring me, I'll make sure your glass gets a refill."

What am I going to do? This is an arrangement I'd like to make, but I can't break character here, not now. Jesus! I can trust Catherine, but can I trust myself to successfully lead a double life? No! No, I can't. I break away from her gaze, look down at the floor, and instinctively look over my shoulder to see who she might be speaking to – my usual gambit.

Catherine lets out a laugh, "That's good!" She leans in and gives me a kiss on my cheek, "Go, and let me know what's going on when you're good and ready."

Now what? All I can think to do is to reach out, shake her hand, and hurry toward the door. From behind I hear her soft voice, "Good night, Doug." My heart is pounding as I rush into the night, across the footbridge, and back to the role that has kept me out of harm's way. Good Lord! That was a close call. Does anyone else know? Does Catherine know, or does she merely suspect? Shit! I don't need this to get any more complicated.

The next morning it's business as usual except for a few men who have been excused to dig the graves in the northwest corner of the Flats, back by the tree line. The nearest priest, Father O'Donnell from Richmond, has come to conduct a service and is in the store meeting with Belknap and Barker when I enter. I go about my usual morning business, and the conversation is fairly benign. The priest is given the names of the deceased and their widows, and informed the widows and their children will be evicted today after the service. Father O'Donnell says he'll offer them temporary shelter.

As the priest rises to leave, the door opens and Sheriff Ferris bounds in, "Good morning, gentlemen! I understand there's been a mishap." The priest quickened his exit without returning the sheriff's greeting. "I need to make certain all deaths are reported and there was no foul play involved; so I need a few minutes of your time."

"Yes. All right, Sheriff," says Belknap, and the sheriff takes Father O'Donnell's chair. Belknap turns his attention to the sheriff, "We lost five men, and they're going to be buried today. I'll give you their particulars for the death certificates."

Ferris straddles an empty chair backwards, resting his arms on the backrest. "Hell, I'm not going to submit death certificates for Patties that aren't citizens, have no legal addresses, and especially if there's no foul play. You don't think there was any foul play, do you? This was just an accident, isn't that right?" Not waiting for an answer, "Accidents happen, so no reason to go through all the trouble of filing death certificates with the county. I'll just talk to a few people and examine the bodies so if the "Free Press" asks me any questions I can answer them."

I don't want to hear any more from that bastard, so as I make my way to the door, it opens, and Mr. O'Reilly and two other men come in, "Can we have a word with you Mr. Belknap?"

Ferris stands up and pushes back his coat exposing his two pistols. "We're meeting here, Patty," Ferris says. "Stay outside until you're invited in." Ferris, recognizing the intruder, "Say, aren't you Murphy's hotheaded friend?"

Belknap, too, stands up and faces Patrick, "Come in. We're finished here, aren't we Sheriff? Yes, come in. I only have a minute." Patrick walks past the sheriff and the sheriff's now empty chair. The two men with Patrick come no further than a few steps in from the door. Neither the sheriff nor I is about to leave, so I go behind the counter and start to wipe it down. But I know I can't do that for long, and Catherine has made me especially cautious about not raising any more suspicion about my ability to hear. So, I change my mind and decide it's best for me to leave. I stop just outside the door pretending to admire the day, yet still able to hear what's going on inside.

"Mr. Belknap," Patrick clears his throat, "We have concerns about the way that trestle is being built. You may know that I am an engineer…"

Belknap breaks in, "What's your name?"

"O'Reilly. Patrick O'Reilly, I'm a civil engineer…"

"Well you're not an engineer here, Mick," Ferris says.

"Sheriff, please. This is our business, says Belknap. "You'd better go out to the grave sites if you want to examine the bodies before they're buried."

The sheriff, having exited, sees me and scowls, "I should arrest you for being stupid, you deaf bastard. What the hell are you good for?" He pushes through the small group of men waiting outside and disappears behind the store. Several of the men turn their gaze back to me, so I give them my idiot smile and nod. On cue, Lucky comes up on the porch, so I sit down, give him a hug, and start petting him. We both look up at our audience; Lucky's dripping tongue draped over his jaw, and my tongue still tied.

A few minutes pass before Mr. O'Reilly emerges with his two cohorts in tow. He addresses the men waiting outside, "They're not going to change the design. Their solution is to tie the God damned joints with rope." Silence… Out of the corner of my eye I see O'Reilly looking down at me, so I glance up, continuing to pet Lucky.

O'Reilly steps off the porch, into the clutch of men. As they start to walk away, I hear a voice from the group, "That might work, Pat. They have as much to lose as we do."

O'Reilly stops and turns to the man, "One life! One life is worth more than that God damned trestle, and we just lost the lives of five men. I'm tired of seeing men die. All they've lost is some time and money. Money? Hell! They haven't even paid us, God damn it!" And off they go.

Work resumed at a subdued pace with some semblance of normal until mid-morning when work stops as if a bell had tolled, although none had. Men and families migrate toward the back corner of the flats for the funeral service. I am with Eggleston when the work stopped and Mr. Freeman approached. I follow them back to the store, and, although I don't go in, I could see in. Barker, Belknap, and Barnum are already inside.

Belknap says, "Let 'em have the service for no more than an hour more. After that I want you," looking at the new arrivals, "to politely tell the men to get back to work. We have to make up for the two weeks' work we lost."

Time for me to disappear, me thinks. So, I head over to the service out of respect, and, too, I still have Catherine's request echoing in my mind: For every bit of important information I bring her, my glass gets a refill! Dare I sell my secret for hard cider? What did Mr. Murphy say? "Having choices is real wealth." Maybe he's right. I should keep the choice of when my hearing comes back to myself for now.

I don't know what I expect to hear at the graveside service. Except for the priest's usual words and an occasional "Amen" and "And peace be with you." The gathering at the gravesides is otherwise silent until the closing prayer is said in unison. I stand in the outer ring of the throng, and the crowd flows around me as the women and children return to their tents and the men to their work. Stoughton has already begun his trip back south, and if he manages to catch the train out of Northfield today, he could be in Connecticut by tomorrow afternoon. The wonders of modern society!

Ten shanks of hemp rope appear at the store following the funeral service, and work to restore the damaged trestle resumes after the midday meal.

Here's an oddity: usually, Murphy's daughter makes her morning trek across the footbridge to Catherine's and comes back well before sunset. But today, after supper and from my perch at the store, I see Mr. Murphy and Christine walking back across the footbridge to Catherine's, and Christine's carrying a something in a sack slung over her shoulder.

We're well into June, so the sun's still up. No else has made his way to Catherine's, but should I head over? Damn! If Catherine believes I can hear, I'm not going to hear anything to make the trip worthwhile. So, here I will sit until later. Where's Lucky?

Chapter 27

GIRLS NIGHT IN

"Father, I haven't spent a night away from you since Mama died." Christine squeezes her father's hand. "But I do like Mrs. Dillon. Are you going to be alright?"

Maury smiles, pulls Christine close, and kisses her forehead as they walk, "Yes, I like Mrs. Dillon, too, and she thinks you're a very special young lady, and you are. I'll be fine. We have a lot going on in camp following the accident, so it's nice thinking of you being safe and sound with Mrs. Dillon. Did you bring your night gown? "

Christine holds up the bulging sack she's carrying, "Father. I'm fourteen. I certainly know what to bring for an overnight stay or two. Will I see you in the morning?"

"Yes, I don't see why not. Or two?" They exchange smiles and go around to Catherine's back entrance. Maury calls inside the open door, "Catherine?" Appearing in the door coming from the tavern, Catherine's wearing a radiant smile as she wipes her hands on her apron.

"Yes, yes, come in!" Catherine grabs Christine's shoulders and gives her a kiss on the cheek. Holding Christine at arm's length and looking directly at her, "Christine, why don't you go up to the loft. I have a cot all set up for you, and I pulled out some empty drawers for you to use."

"I'll wait for you to come down, Sweetheart," Maury says as Christine throws her satchel through the opening at the top of the ladder and follows it up to the loft without looking back.

Maury's eyes stay on the ladder until Christine disappears, and he then turns to Catherine. Walking over to where she stands, he gently holds her shoulders and moves her back against the cupboard at the far end of the kitchen and presses his body against hers. Catherine yields to Maury's initiative. How refreshing, she thinks, to be joyfully expectant and willfully compliant. Fixing his gaze on Catherine's moist lips, Maury's hand lifts her chin to bring her open mouth closer to his. Leaning in he kisses her once, then again. Brief, gentle kisses; one and then another and another until her passion is unleashed. Embracing him fully, her hand at the back of Maury's head, she does not let his lips leave hers. Their passion is ignited, and it seems to consume all the oxygen in the room, quickly leaving them both breathless.

They pause to take in the moment, and slowly their arms drop until each is holding the other's hands. They stand facing each other in silence; foreheads touching. A moment passes, and Catherine resumes drying utensils and says, "I'll see Christine goes to bed at sundown, and tonight should be a quiet night in the tavern so she won't hear much if anything up in the loft. It doesn't share a wall with the tavern."

"She's been looking forward to this evening ever since I passed on your invitation," says Maury. "You've been so nice to her, Catherine, and you have become a very special person in her life; in both of our lives. She misses her mother, but less so now." As he says it, he realizes this was probably not a good time to bring his departed wife into the room. "She talks about those chickens like they're her own."

Catherine turns and with a knowing look, touches Maury's arm and says, "Come by later to see how she's doing and kiss her good night."

Before he could answer, Christine's feet appear on the ladder, and down she comes barely touching the rungs, "Oh, Father, the loft is lovely! You must see it! There's a chest of drawers, a big metal bed, and a braided rug covers the whole floor. I have my own drawer, and there's a glass window that opens!"

Maury goes to the ladder and up several rungs until just his head pokes above the floor and he can see into the loft. The evening sun is coming in a hinged, four pane window, opened slightly, set high in the far wall. Against the near wall a beam of evening light falls on a finely made chest of drawers topped by a mirror reflecting the sunlight back into the room. On a small table with a finely padded stool under it, Maury can see the glint of a silver hair brush and a number of cut glass bottles; items that would belong to the wife of a successful merchant. He steps back down the ladder.

"It's a beautiful room. I'll come back at sundown to say 'good night', Christine."

"Yes, do, father." And Christine scampers back up the ladder.

Maury turns to Catherine, "I'll be back in a bit, Catherine." With that said, he leaves through the back door, crosses the footbridge, and returns to his tent where he sees Patrick.

"Aye, Patrick!" says Maury, and seeing Kathleen, her head just emerging from the tent, "Good evening, Madam."

"You seem particularly well, Maury," says Kathleen.

Not waiting for confirmation, Patrick says, "I had no luck with management. The only change the bastards are going to make is to tie the joints with rope. Rope! It'll stretch when it gets wet. Why don't they just do it right? Damn it!"

"Pat, I think the best decision we can make is for us to go back to work." Maury turns to glance at Catherine's establishment and then west to see how close the sun is to going down behind the mountains. "Let's see how well the fix works, and if we see it's not going to work, then we can decide what to do."

"I have at least twenty-five men that are willing to refuse to work…"

Maury cuts him off mid-sentence, "Refusing to work will only get you fired and replaced by twenty-five more poor souls as desperate as we were two months ago."

"They haven't paid us, they've killed five of us, eight if you count the men in the woods, and they've shown no mercy for the widows and their fatherless children. They should be arrested." Patrick is still furious. "They're picking us off like crockery on a fence rail."

"Yeah? And who's going to arrest them? Ferris? He's more likely to arrest you for complaining." Maury again turns toward the setting sun.

"What are you looking at?" asks Patrick. "And where's Christine?"

Kathleen's voice comes from inside the O'Reilly's tent, "She's staying with Catherine tonight. That's all she talked about this afternoon."

"Yes, and I'm going to go back after sunset and give her a kiss good night. We've never spent a night apart," says Maury.

Patrick's face lights up, "And just how many women are you going to kiss good night, Mr. Murphy?"

"Patrick! Don't you tease Mr. Murphy," scolds Kathleen.

"Why, I thought you didn't like her, Katy." Kathleen comes out of their tent, and aims a "watch what you say" stare at Patrick.

"I had my doubts at first, but she and Christine are quite close, and from everything Christine has told me, I have a growing respect for her. And you, Mr. O'Reilly, had better be nice to me, or I might have the sheriff cart you off, too!" Kathleen kisses Patrick's cheek and retreats back into the tent.

Maury, again glances west, "I have a few things to do before saying 'good night' to Christine." Maury returns to his tent and goes inside. After quite awhile, he emerges, buttoning a clean shirt over which he puts on a coat he has not worn since arriving in the camps. Noting the last sliver of sun has disappeared, leaving a golden glow above the mountains, he turns toward the O'Reilly tent and departs saying to no one present, "Well! It's about time for me to check on Christine and say 'good night'."

From inside the O'Reilly tent, "I'll join you later, Maury." That stops Maury in his tracks. After a moment, and hearing no response, Patrick says, "Well, if I don't see you tonight, Maury, I'll see you in the morning."

Chapter 28

GOOD NIGHT LADIES

On this rare rainless night, the full moon lights our way as Barnum, Barker, Lucky, and I head across the footbridge to Catherine's with Mr. Murphy close behind. Barnum and Barker enter the tavern first, then Lucky, but as I hold the door open for Mr. Murphy, he tips his hat and continues around to the back of the building. Ha! What's going on? The scoundrel!!

Inside, I'm surprised to see Mr. Strong, the blacksmith from Jonesville, behind the bar. Considering the mood of the camp, I didn't expect the tavern to be busy enough for Catherine to secure extra help. Ah! Catherine must be expecting to spend some time with Mr. Murphy. What a good time to be invisible! I stand at the bar close to the door to the backroom hoping Barnum will choose to stand there, too, so I might hear what is otherwise going in the back room. But no. After getting a rum for himself and hard cider for me, he motions me over to a table. Lucky finds a spot to lie down, and we sit one table away from the only other two men in the room. Their conversation stops as we approach. A few minutes later others wander in, and muted talk barely breaks the silence.

When Catherine appears from the back room in a ruffled white skirt, white blouse and shawl with her blond hair pulled back, Lucky gets up and goes right over and sits at her feet; looking up and waging his tail. I was tempted to do the same.

Catherine whispers something to Mr. Strong, he nods, and as she turns to return to the back room, Lucky get up to follow. Normally,

Catherine would let Lucky tag along just about anywhere, but not this time. She bends down, rubs behind his ears with both hands, and says something to him under her breath. Lucky turns his head toward me, then back to watch Catherine as she disappears into the back. Lucky returns to his spot at my feet. Lucky's look of resignation echoes my feelings exactly. I know, Boy. What a good time to be invisible!

Maury enters Catherine's back door. "After you say 'good night' to Christine, let's take a walk," says Catherine. "I've packed a picnic."

"That sounds nice," says Maury, and he disappears up the ladder to the loft. The room is illuminated by an oil lamp under which Christine is lying in the cot with a book in her hands. She smiles when she sees her father's head appear poking up through the floor.

"Father! Look at this. It's a seed catalogue from Holland. Can you read it to me? Look at all these different kinds of flowers."

Maury crawls up on the loft's floor toward where his daughter is holding out a paper book. He lifts the tattered volume from his daughter's hand. "I'm afraid it's in Dutch, Sweetheart, and I can't read Dutch."

Leafing through several pages he holds a page up for Christine to see. "Do you recognize this one?"

"Yes, that's a tulip! Look at how it's spelled, Papa: T-U-L-P. And there's another word under it: she spelled out B-L-O-E-M-S-O-O-R-T. Bloom-sort?"

"Must be. That certainly is a tulip. Now it's time to go to sleep. Are you ready?"

"Yes. This bed is so comfortable, and the pillow is full of feathers! Are you going to miss me? Will you come see me in the morning?"

"Yes. I'll check on you later before I return to camp, and I'll come see you tomorrow before I begin work. Ok?" Maury leans down and kisses Christine's forehead before he turns down the wick in the lamp, extinguishing the flame. The light in the room fades from a warm yellow to a soft blue-white as the mild June air and moonlight come in on a soft breeze through the open window.

Maury descends the ladder from the loft. Catherine has a basket on the counter. She folds an oilcloth and places it on top of the basket's contents. "I thought we could take a walk on this beautiful night. It will be quiet here, and I asked John to keep an ear to the back in case Christine awakens. We won't go far, but I do know of a small clearing part way up the hill where we can sit. John knows to call out back if we're needed."

"That sounds just fine, Catherine." Maury can feel his heart quicken, aware that this will be the first time he and Catherine will be truly alone.

"Here. Let me take that," he says as he lifts the heavy basket. Catherine leads the way out the back door. Once outside, Catherine puts one arm through his, resting her other hand on his muscled forearm as they begin their trek up the mountain trail. The moon is bright enough to light a well-worn path from the clearing around the boardinghouse up into the woods. Upon reaching a slight plateau Catherine guides them onto a side path leading to a small, grassy area with a downed tree bordering the uphill side of the clearing; an inviting place to sit and look out over the valley below dotted with small campfires.

"This is very nice, Catherine," says Maury admiring their private spot in the woods, obviously a product of her handy work. Setting the basket down he feels Catherine's hand on his back. Catherine reaches down, and unfolds the oilcloth; spreading it on the ground. Maury kneels and thoughtfully, somewhat reverently, smoothes it out.

As Maury rises, he turns to see Catherine, her white ensemble glowing in the moonlight. He steps forward and takes Catherine in his arms. They kiss, pause, and kiss again; this time long, sustained, and passionate. Maury's fingers slide up to the curve of Catherine's neck. Catherine unpins her hair, and shakes her head to let it fall to her shoulders and frame her upturned face. Maury feels the whole of Catherine's body pressing against his, and she freely yields to his powerful embrace as they kiss. At that moment their universe is wholly within this clearing.

The haunting hoot of an owl brings them back to their worldly place and time, yet still quite separate from the camps and boardinghouse below. The couple slowly disentwine; their embrace giving way to holding hands, and then together making a place to share the evening and the contents of Catherine's basket. She removes her shawl, exposing her partially unbuttoned blouse, and she reclines on the oilcloth, leaning on one arm. With the other she takes from the basket a warm loaf of bread, hard goat cheese wrapped in waxed paper, and a blue ceramic flagon with two matching mugs.

"This, Mr. Murphy, is five year old whiskey, the best whiskey the Canadians produce." The moonlight shimmers on her hair and adds a twinkle to her green eyes now raised to look up at Maury who has folded his coat carefully and placed it on a corner of their impromptu tablecloth.

Maury sits facing Catherine, and as she fills their mugs, his gaze wanders from her pale ankles emerging from under her ruffled skirt, past her cinched waist, to her loose-fitting blouse and the hint of her breasts now only partially covered. "You are a beautiful woman," says Maury.

"And you, dear man, are not only handsome, but also a very good father." Catherine hands Maury a mug. "A toast. May the warmth of our affection survive the frosts of life in the North Woods!"

Maury, smiling, adds, "Amen!" And they drink, their eyes locked on each other.

Their hushed conversation is punctuated by gentle laughter as they eat and empty the flagon. Hanging directly overhead, the nearly full moon lights the forest. "It's cooling down, Catherine, would you like your shawl?" Without waiting for an answer, he rises to get her shawl, and Catherine rises with him. Standing close enough for Maury to be aware of her scent, Catherine brings her hand up to her blouse, pauses, and unbuttons one, and then the next and the next until her open blouse exposes the pale, smooth flesh of her softly sculpted torso. As Maury bows to kiss her, Catherine puts one finger to Maury's lips and straightens him up.

With two hands, Catherine unbuttons Maury's shirt, and opening it wide, she puts her warm hands on his chest and places a lingering kiss between them. With his eyes closed, Maury lifts his head to the sky, savoring the sensation of Catherine's gentle touch. This precious moment hangs in the air as Catherine takes a half step back, and a breeze catches her open top slipping it off of her shoulder. The sight of Catherine's bare breast unleashes all of the passion that has been building in Maury. He removes his shirt, brushes Catherine's blouse off her other shoulder, and it falls to the ground next to his. He takes her fully in his arms, and bringing her down to the cloth-covered ground, both are overwhelmed by the power of their unbridled passion.

Unaware of how much time had passed, they laid still, each embraced by the other, breathless, and looking up at the splash of stars growing brighter as the moon starts its descent.

The couple returned to the now dark boardinghouse under the last of the night's moonlight. After checking to see that Christine was sound asleep, Maury and Catherine had one last kiss before he made his way back to camp. The next morning, before the day's work began, Maury appears at Catherine's back door. Before he could knock, Christine opens the door and throws her arms around her father and says, "I made you breakfast, Papa. Eggs and potatoes! Do you have time?"

"I do, Sweetheart." Stepping inside, Catherine is standing there to greet him, wiping her hands on her apron.

"Good morning, Mr. Murphy," she says with a wink. "Did you have a good night's sleep?"

"Indeed I did, Mrs. Dillon." So much to say, but this isn't the time to say it. Looking at the table, Maury sees three plates, each with two fried eggs and a golden cake of fried potatoes. "I haven't seen potatoes worth eating in quite awhile," says Maury, and they sit together and break their night's fast before Maury heads back across the footbridge to do his day's work.

Chapter 29

A MILESTONE REACHED

Two weeks after the calamity that took the lives of five men and crippled two more, the trestle has been repaired, unlike the trust between the railroad and its crew. When the trestle reached halfway across the river, bent construction moved to the south side. Today we expect to drop the last bent into place while work continues on the rail bed on the south side of the river.

As the final bents are being constructed some of the loggers felling and preparing timber for the bents have been assigned to the substructure tying the joints – a fool's errand to the now skeptical crew. Mr. Murphy and several others have the new responsibility of moving the milled lumber used for the braces and stringers to the trestle and passing whatever is needed up to the men working in the structure.

It became apparent to those working in the trestle that Mr. Stoughton didn't anticipate the constant vibrations from the flow of the river and occasional flotsam loosening the spiked joints. Several men are constantly busy making repairs and tying and re-tying the ropes being used to keep the joints intact. To make matters worse, once a spike is loosened, it doesn't have quite the same grip after it's hammered back in. But by lashing the joints and covering the spikes with rope, I heard Freeman argue, that degradation is addressed. Not all agreed.

I hear the managers say among themselves that it's fortunate we haven't lost additional life or limb since the accident. Fewer men have chosen to tether themselves to the structure, so several times a day a worker is dunked in the river after loosing his footing on the slick surfaces. This June, in fact the entire spring, has seen much more rain than last year. The only way to dry clothes is to hang them over the fires to dry, absorbing the acrid wood smoke, and the sharp, unpleasant smell of smoke clings to each man, woman, and child throughout the day and into the next.

Although we had no rain yesterday, clouds are gathering. It's late June and yet it simply hasn't stopped raining, and the clouds of biting flies are at their worst. Men work with kerchiefs over the mouths to keep from inhaling the swarms around every head. By this time last year the ground between the tents was dry, work was on schedule, and the men had been paid most of what was owed them. But not this year. We're behind schedule, the entire worksite is still muddy, and the men haven't seen half their wages.

Worker debt has been accumulating at the company store, and the familiar and unpleasant feeling of being indentured to an unsympathetic master weighs on the spirit of those who for generations have suffered in the bondage of debt in spite of the fact the railroad generally owes them more than they owe the railroad. Some worry the railroad holds the official record of debits and credits, and it all feels too much like the oppressive society we left behind. The Brits controlled the money, the land, and the government, and the railroad controls the money, the land, and our food and shelter. And to make matters worse that bastard sheriff appears to be the only government we have for miles around.

Mr. Stoughton arrived last night on the supply train. This time, just as the last, he is reassuring us the structure will be stable and secure, especially once it's anchored to the far shore, and today is the day we should reach that milestone. For several days men had been working on the opposite bank preparing the approach that will anchor the trestle. They have been laying blocks of granite on the ground to form the foundation that will receive the weight of an iron steam engine coming off the trestle.

Timbers have been sunk into the ground to which braces will be attached tying the trestle to the far bank. Once that's done, stringers will be laid from the trestle to the foundation, and ties will be laid across the stringers. Then all that will be left to do is to lay the tracks across the trestle, spike them to the ties, and continue laying ties and rails on the new bed heading to Jonesville and the world beyond.

Word got around that a few company board members are going to be arriving to survey our progress. It certainly would change the general mood of the camps if they bring the rest of the payroll with them. Not likely, though. Whenever they've come up in the past, they stay near the company offices in Northfield or in Montpelier to glad-hand the politicians. After a brief visit to the worksite they are quick to return to the comforts of home. While the supervisors have confirmed that board members would be here to inspect our work, they also are quick to caution the workers not to badger board members about the missed payrolls.

"Yes," they say, "the board knows cash has been short, and yes, they regret it. But they are doing their best to raise the cash, and it won't do any good to complain about it," and so on.

I have heard hushed debate among some of the crews about whether or not to take some action, but moderate views seem to have won the day. Of course, it only takes one angry man to make a scene. But, in general, the men seem to have taken great pride in their accomplishments and simply are anxious to be praised by their overlords. Kinda like Lucky getting an "atta boy" and a pat on the head after retrieving a downed partridge. Of course, that was before the accident that took him and me out of the game.

The pace quickens as the final bent is dropped into place, and a cheer goes up as the stringers from the top of the trestle are spiked to the timbers sunk in the foundation on the far bank. Stoughton watches from his perch beside Belknap while Barnum and Freeman, on the far side, direct work there. Mr. Stoughton calls Barker over and instructs him to assign any extra men to the trestle and to supervise the final securing of the trestle's joints over the next few days.

By midday thickening clouds begin to drop rain on the valley, keeping footing among the trestle's timbers unsure for the nearly thirty men still working within and on top of the trestle. To accomplish their work they must climb all about the structure, hammering in loosened spikes and tying and re-tying hundreds of joints.

At the end of the day, Lucky and I tag along with Barker and Barnum as they head for Catherine's. Footing is unsure on the well-worn foot-bridge made even more treacherous by the river running so high that occasionally waves slap the upriver side and spill over the surface. The distant sound of high spirits and laughter soon overcome the sound of rain and thunder as we approach the welcoming glow of the tavern where there is standing room only. Lucky has no choice but to go around to the back of the building. Catherine has moved all of the tables against the walls to accommodate the extra bodies and has brought in Mr. Strong to help. Seems like the entire camp is here tonight. Not only is there some-thing to celebrate, but the storm building throughout the day is unleashing a constant downpour punctuated by booming thunder and sharp flashes of lightning. Catherine's is a welcome refuge from the storm.

Everyone has grown accustomed to seeing Mr. Murphy's daughter here during the day, but more than one head turns when Christine peaks out from behind the door to Catherine's living quarters. Mr. Murphy likes to stand near the end of the bar so that he can have frequent contact with Catherine throughout the night, so when O'Reilly sees Christine's head come around the edge of the door his elbow jabs Mr. Murphy, and he nods toward Christine. Mr. Murphy hands O'Reilly his drink and goes into the back room.

Catherine, who doesn't miss a trick, follows Mr. Murphy into the back. I have to know what's going on behind that door, so I leave the company of Barnum and Barker and casually make my way over next to O'Reilly, but with my back to him so not to be too obvious. Don't mind me, Patrick ol' boy! The deaf guy is just standing here looking around like I've not a care in the world, and you be sure to ask Mr. Murphy what the hell is going on behind that closed door!

Catherine emerges, makes a tour of the room, and checks in with Mr. Strong behind the bar. Then Catherine goes into the back once again. More minutes pass, and as Catherine reappears she has pulled her hair back into a bun and is smoothing her dress. Moments later Mr. Murphy comes in the side door from the outside and takes his place next to O'Reilly. They exchange smiles. Mr. Murphy tells O'Reilly he put Christine to bed. Yes? And what else, Mr. Murphy? Come on, man, we want details!

But O'Reilly doesn't ask the questions I have in mind. No more details are forthcoming. Their conversation turns to the trestle, the missed payrolls, the rain, the mud, and the relentless insects; and only after a pause does O'Reilly ask Mr. Murphy about his visit with Catherine last evening. Yes? Yes? Mr. Murphy looks down at his drink, and then over to Catherine and back to O'Reilly.

"Catherine prepared a nice basket with bread and cheese and some excellent Canadian whiskey. After I put Christine to bed, Catherine and I walked up into the woods behind the house to a nice clearing in the woods." Mr. Murphy took a slow sip.

Come on, Man!! Don't stop now!

"And...?" asks O'Reilly, curious as I to hear more.

Mr. Murphy continues, "Well, we took advantage of a beautiful night, and realized how much we are attracted to each other." He pauses, looks into his glass, and then up again. Smiling, he says, "It was a special evening. I haven't felt this way since I first courted Christine's mother, so many years ago."

I'm not hearing any details, Man!

"I'm very happy for you, Maury," says O'Reilly as he puts his free hand on Maury's shoulder. "Anything else you want to share with your good friend?"

Yes, Man. Share!!

Maury pauses, and finally says, "It was a very special night, my friend!" And he lifts his glass as if making a toast of thanks to God.

"Atta boy!" declares O'Reilly. "I'm happy for you, Maury...and for Christine." And just as he said that, I must have lost my invisibility because they both turn toward me.

I return their glance, give them my "everything is fine" doggy smile, and look around as if I had heard nothing. I guess O'Reilly and I will have to be content with "a special night." So this evening passes as others had: with song and camaraderie until several of the men who had just departed return and with a degree of panic in their voices and announce that the river is nearly washing over the footbridge, and anyone returning to the camp side had better leave now.

A voice from the room bellows, "Abandon ship!" and round of laughter follows the directive. The tavern empties as fast as the mugs and glasses can be drained. Barnum and Barker are among the first to leave. O'Reilly and Mr. Murphy leave after they both say "good night" to Catherine, with Maury adding he'd be back in the morning. I follow them out, and sure enough, the river is six inches short of over-topping the bridge. The wind, torrential downpour, and the slippery surface of the bridge combine to make the crossing so treacherous that several men cross on hands and knees. More than one man loses his footing, but, luckily, no one falls into the rushing water.

Chapter 30

NATURE PLAYS NINE PIN

The torrential rain and gale force winds diminish overnight, ending by daybreak. But heavy, dark gray, low-hanging clouds still blanket the valley. I have never seen the river so high and fast this late in the year. It's now flowing over the top of the footbridge making it impassable, but we do have the trestle in place, so management ordered the crew working on the far side to cross using the trestle and resume work after taking their morning meal. Rousted early, thirty or so men assigned to the trestle are already making their way through the substructure with shanks of rope over their shoulders, knives on their belts, and hammers in hand. Each pair assigned to a bent.

The unrelenting force of the swollen river is shaking the trestle, even though it's solidly anchored to God's good earth and the well-laid granite foundations at both ends. For those men used to walking and working on solid ground it's a bit tricky for them to walk across the slick, newly laid stringers on top of the vibrating trestle, but it appears to be more of an amusement than a danger. Belknap says the important task for the next two days, now that the structure's in place, will be to stabilize it by re-wrapping and tightening the ropes at each of the several hundred spiked joints.

I'm in the company store when I overhear Belknap tell Barnum and Stoughton that Vice Chairman Rake and at least two other members of the board will be here in the morning to inspect our progress.

"They should be satisfied that we have repaired the trestle and are back on schedule," comments Belknap. "How does it look to you, Mr. Stoughton?"

Stoughton, with a seemingly high degree of confidence says, "Now that the trestle is anchored to both banks I don't see any reason we can't start laying the rails across the trestle after the joints are tightened. Once we run an engine across, the trestle will be fully settled in the riverbed, and ready for operation. I've ordered a load of rails, and they should be delivered in four or five days, so full steam ahead!" His fist punches the sky.

Belknap is pleased. "Good! Good! Now if we can just…"

Panicked shouts from outside interrupt Belknap. He gets up so quickly he up-ends his chair, and as he reaches for the door, Eggleston bursts in nearly knocking him over. "Come quick!!! We may have a problem."

Rushing outside and standing on the store's front porch we can see men moving toward the bank and pointing up river. Several hundred yards upstream is a mass of debris tumbling and rolling end over end in the middle of the boiling current. The trestle, acting as a sieve across the river, has already collected some flotsam, but nothing as threatening as the approaching menace. Some of the men on top of the trestle are frozen in their tracks; others have dropped to their hands and knees and are crawling to one end of the trestle or the other. Two men have lost their footing and have fallen into the water. Freeman is yelling for everyone to stay where they are and to hold on. Several men in the substructure not tethered start to tie themselves to the nearest timber.

We rush toward the trestle, pushing through the gathering crowd on shore. The oncoming mass appears to be a beaver dam that was lifted and freed from its mooring by the rising waters of one of the Onion's tributaries, and now it's in the main channel rushing toward the trestle like a bowling ball toward nine pins. Nearly everyone on shore is yelling, "Get down from there," or "Hold on! Hold on!" The cries of women closest to the river start to join the panic; some crossing their breasts and praying, others running this way and that. A half dozen men make it to shore safely, but there are still ten or so on top and nearly thirty in the substructure as the mass of trees, brush, rocks, and dried mud takes direct aim at the trestle.

Without slowing down, the bludgeon strikes the trestle, splintering the two center bents, collapsing the center and drawing the rest of the structure in and down toward the site of impact. Cries of agony are mixed with the prolonged and repeated crack of the timbers as they give way to the irresistible power of the water pinning the dam against the broken timbers. Six or seven men on top and several in the substructure are thrown into the water. Two disappear under the water and the others are collected by the now flooded footbridge and lifted to safety.

I look back at the trestle, and to my horror I see a torso stuck in the timbers made headless by two crossed braces that have sheared the head from the body. I watch as the orphaned head tumbles toward the footbridge where it is dragged under by the current and pops out on the downstream side continuing its way to Lake Champlain. Other bodies, crushed by the collapsing structure, hang lifeless above the current. The trestle continues to collapse as the river pushes against the trapped dam until what remains of the trestle finally settles into a tangle of timbers and boards dropping one lifeless body into the water and trapping more than twenty others still alive and terrified.

Two men are able to extricate themselves by pulling their broken limbs out of the wreckage, and they make their way to shore. Several men climb onto the jumble of timbers to aid the escape of those still trapped, but are frustrated in their efforts. The weight of the collapsed structure holds on tightly to those still trapped in the tangle. Belknap, Barker, Barnum, Eggleston, and Freeman stand together surveying the destruction.

"Jesus Christ!" says Freeman. "What can we do?"

Belknap, seeing that the trestle may continue to collapse, yells to the men who have climbed onto the trestle to rescue those trapped, "Get down from there!" Turning to the others, he commands, "Eggleston and Freeman, get some timbers and prop up what remains of the trestle. Go!"

Eggleston grabs my arm as he heads to the trestle. Pointing to a small group of men stunned by what they had just witnessed, Eggleston gets their attention, "You, all of you, bring two timbers over here to prop up the trestle. Freeman, get some men and take timbers to the other side and do the same."

The stunned men didn't move. "Now!!" he barks.

Within several minutes, one group has retrieved a timber and wedged it between the topmost piece of the trestle's frame and the ground. Several stakes were driven in at its base to keep it from slipping; halting the structure's continuing collapse from the river's constant pressure. Across the river, the men were not as quick, and the far side had collapsed further and had come to settle on its own.

Seeing the disintegration of the trestle has been halted, Belknap approaches Barker, "I want you to organize a group of men to care for those still trapped. See what can be done for them – food, water, and tend to their wounds. Do not try to remove or dislodge any of the structure or the whole thing could come apart and take everyone down with it. Get the names of the dead still trapped in the structure."

Turning to Barnum, Belknap says, "Find Stoughton and meet me at the store. Go among the work crews and reassure them that we are going to do everything we can to rescue those still trapped. Listen to their ideas, but don't promise anything. Nothing. Do you understand?" Belknap pans the wide eyes of his subordinates staring at him, "Got it?" And seeing no reaction, he claps his hands, "Ok, let's go. Now! Go! Go!"

The men went to execute their assignments, and I am invisible once more. I go over to where the men are gathered at the foot of the trestle, and stand looking at the cataclysm near where Mr. O'Reilly is holding court with a dozen other men, "We told them it wasn't sound; it wasn't going to hold up, and now look what's happened."

Barnum sees the group and approaches, "We have a situation that needs everyone's cooperation."

O'Reilly, his anger unleashed, is first to speak, "Yeah? What cooperation do you need from us? We've already cooperated by building that damned thing the way we were told. I'll tell ya what we should do. We need to start dismantling that damned thing right away, piece by piece, and try to save as many of the men trapped as soon as possible. When can we get started?"

Barnum holds up his hands, "Whoa! Stop. We're going to be meeting with the engineer in a few minutes to determine the best course of action. Do not do anything until we have a plan to move forward. Move one timber and the whole thing could come apart. We are assembling a crew to give aid to those trapped in the trestle. If you want to help, go see Eggleston and Freeman." Barnum points to the two supervisors as he makes his way to the next group.

I leave Barnum and make my way back to the store through a sea of people running in all directions. The cries for help coming from the men trapped in what was once the trestle are constant. On shore, women and children are in tears, begging whomever will listen to do something, but nothing more can be done. Those injured and on shore are getting aid; Barker is organizing others to attend to those still trapped; and Belknap is standing at the store's entrance placating a group of men and women demanding action and answers. As I approach, he waves me to come inside with him, perhaps concerned for my safety.

I busy myself ripping cotton cloth into strips for bandages and tourniquets, and I use the rod from a bolt of the cloth to fashion a torch to be used for stopping the bleeding from the amputations that seem inevitable.

In the store Belknap and Stoughton are soon in a tense conversation. Stoughton is panicked, "Board members are due here tomorrow, and I don't know what to tell them. I mean, we couldn't predict that something like this could happen, could we? If we had had just one more day, just one more day, the trestle could have withstood the blow. Dear God! It was bad timing. Just bad timing..."

"Pull yourself together, man. They're going to want our recommendations, Phillip. What are our options?"

Stoughton begins to focus, "Well, we could start construction of another trestle while we disassemble the old one. Of course, that would mean we have to move the rail bed on both sides of the river to meet the new trestle. Or, we could simply disassemble the old trestle and rebuild in place," offers Stoughton. "What else can we do?"

Belknap leaves Stoughton's question unanswered. After a moment of reflection, Belknap says, "In either case we'll need some answers. If we dismantle the trestle, how long will that take? Then the question that needs to be answered is: do we rebuild using the same design and materials, or do we go back to the standard method of using milled timbers and bolts? What do you think?"

"Honestly?" asks Stoughton. He looks over his shoulder and sees no one but me as I'm busy collecting items to take out to the trestle, "Just between you and me, our shortcut was no shortcut at all, as it turned out. But that was because of the heavy spring rains. This shouldn't have happened. It's just bad timing…just bad timing."

Obviously losing his patience, Belknap repeats his question "So what is your recommendation, Phillip?"

"Sweet Jesus! I don't know." Stoughton holds his head in his hands. Looking up he says, "Ok, ok, I'd recommend disassembling the trestle, re-building where it now stands, and going back to the old method of using milled timbers and bolting the joints. We know it works and works well. All of that can be completed by mid-August, and we may reach our goal for the season if the snow holds off."

"All right, then. I want you here in the morning when the board members arrive," says Belknap, "and I will agree with you. We will recommend dismantling the trestle and constructing its replacement where it now stands using milled timbers and bolts. Those supplies can be here by the time the old trestle is disassembled, and in the meantime, let's see what we can do for the injured."

Belknap and Stoughton stand and shake hands. I follow Stoughton out with bandages, a saw, and the unlit torch in hand. Across the river I see Catherine standing with her arm around Christine's shoulder, and Christine's father, separated from them by the rushing water, is waving to them both.

The injured are being cared for and the widows consoled. Groups of men are scattered around the worksite in intense conversations. Some are pointing to the trestle, others pointing at the store. Throughout the night, sleep is difficult or impossible as the sounds of distress from the trestle continue. Who can sleep hearing the cries and painful moans of those trapped in the railroad's monstrosity? I certainly can't, so I wander from group to group, wholly invisible, hearing talk ranging from simply quitting and leaving the worksite, to confronting management, demanding changes in how the trestle is constructed, and full pay before they return to work. Exhausted, I sit on the store's porch and fall into an uneasy sleep.

Chapter 31

THE BOARD ARRIVES

Dawn broke, faintly lighting the groups of men huddled around campfires lining the riverbank. Water and nourishment are being given to those still trapped in the trestle. The water level has receded just enough so the footbridge is back in use, and two of the first across are Catherine and Christine carrying an ample supply of alcohol to ease the pain of the injured.

Two men chose to be freed by amputating their trapped limbs – one mangled leg and a crushed arm. Tourniquets were applied last night, and Belknap will do the amputations. He has a surgical kit in a magnificent mahogany case with shiny brass hinges and clasp. He's quite proud of it. Inside are long, shiny curved knives with bone handles for cutting flesh and muscle and two different saws for cutting bone. Beautiful tools for a gruesome task. After an ax had inflicted a large wound in a worker's foot last year, the wound failed to heal and his limb started to turn green and black. Belknap amputated the calf and foot. The man survived long enough to be put on a stage west.

I hear Belknap tell the wives of the current victims that both amputations should take place above a joint; one above the elbow, the other above the knee. He asks each of the men affected if he wants an ax to do the job quickly, or if they want him to use the surgical kit to leave enough muscle to cover the bone and enough flesh to fold over and close the open wound. Both men choose the more careful and prolonged surgical amputation to improve their odds of survival. So, after they are given a substantial amount of Catherine's alcohol, Belknap climbs into the tangle of timber with his kit in hand and skillfully amputates the limbs, freeing the men and leaving their orphaned limbs pinned in the trestle.

Several women in the camp, members of a Catholic order dedicated to the care and recuperation of the sick and injured, sew up the incisions once the men are brought to the riverbank. All the injured who manage to get off the trestle are recuperating in their tents. Eggleston directs others to begin the task of digging more graves in what is now a consecrated graveyard in the northwest corner of the Flats.

Not long afterward, that son-of-a-bitch sheriff appears on the Stage Road coming from the west on horseback carrying something swinging from his left hand. He pauses at the sight of the collapsed trestle and the men trapped within it, both dead and alive. Some onlookers are horrified to see that the sheriff is carrying the severed head. He crosses the footbridge still mounted, ties his horse to the hitching post in front of the store, and places the head on the porch facing the trestle. What the hell is he doing here? He pays no attention to me as I enter the store behind him.

Seeing Belknap and Barker, Ferris brightens as he greets them, "Good morning, gentlemen. Looks like you've had another accident." Both turned to see who has entered, but neither responds. Ferris continues, "I thought something was amiss when a man reported a human head trapped in some branches down river. So I came to see what happened, and to return the damned thing for burial. What did happen, and what the hell are you going to do now?'"

"We're just talking about that, Sheriff," says Belknap, "and I'd appreciate you wiping that fucking smirk of your face before you go back outside. In fact, wipe it off right now. We're trying to determine how many men we've lost, and what we're going to do going forward. We have board members due up here any minute, and they're going to want answers. Is there something we can do for you?"

"No, no. Just tell me there was no foul play, and I'll report the number of deaths to the coroner as accidental deaths."

"There was no foul play, Sheriff," says Belknap. "The high water busted the trestle, and we're doing our best to take care of the injured and remove the trapped men. You're welcome to stay and talk to folks, but please be respectful of the situation. We have at least seven dead and many more injured. I should be able to give you a final count by the end of the day."

"I understand, Henry," says Ferris, hat in hand. "I don't mean to be disrespectful. Just doin' my job. I'll be here all day, and maybe pay a visit to Mrs. Dillon later. I'll be sure to check back with you before I leave." Apparently, no one has anything else to say, and the two men just stare at the sheriff as he backs toward the door and exits, closing the door behind him.

"I'd like to punch that bastard in the nose," says Barker.

The door opens just as Belknap adds, "You'll have to stand in line, John," and Barnum's head appears.

"The train from Northfield's coming in, Mr. Belknap," announces Barnum. We all follow Barnum out. The train stops a hundred yards short of what once was the trestle. Belknap, Barker, and Barnum run at a trot to the single passenger car trailing the engine and coal car while Eggleston directs the men who are drawn toward the approaching train to unload supplies from the boxcar.

Vice-chairman Rake appears first. He jumps down from the car, followed by board members Michael Adams and Treasurer Mazer. As they walk from behind the engine Rake stops dead in his tracks. He can see the offending beaver damn still pinned against the partially collapsed structure. "What the fuck is going on, Belknap? Jesus Christ, man, what the hell happened?"

Belknap is contrite, "Well, sir, the heavy rains this spring have caused a lot of damage, and just yesterday…"

Rake cuts him off mid-sentence, "Yesterday? Let me ask you a more important question: what the hell are you doing about it today?" Rake starts to slowly walk in the direction of the trestle with Adams and Mazer close behind.

Mr. Adams pushes his way to the front of the entourage, and jumps in front of Belknap, stopping him, "Mr. Belknap, do you have a plan for getting those men out?"

Belknap seems relieved to be answering Mr. Adams' questions, "Yes, sir, yes, sir, we do. We have a gang caring for the men trapped in the timbers, and we are going to begin to get them out this morning. The plan is to save what material we can and rebuild at the existing site."

Unable to contain his anger, Rake takes Belknap by one arm and spins him around so they are face to face, "I don't give a God damn about the materials, Belknap. I care about time. Materials can be bought, and men can be replaced, but time is priceless."

Mr. Stoughton appears, hat in hand, as Rake and the others approach the trestle's north foundation. Rake, seeing a sledgehammer leaning up against the single temporary support holding up what remains of the trestle, picks it up, and holds it up in front of him like a scepter; or as if he is taking aim at the tangled timbers. After a long moment he drops the heavy hammer onto his shoulder. Belknap pulls Stoughton next to him, "Well, sir, that's why we…," Belknap looks at Stoughton and pulls him to his side, "… that's why we recommend re-building the trestle at the same location so we don't have to relocate the rail bed and approaches. Isn't that right, Phillip?"

Rake, not waiting for Stoughton's response, "Of course we'll rebuild where the trestle is now. Too much time will be wasted if we have to relocate the rail bed. So when can we start rebuilding?" Rake looks around for someone to give him the answer he wants to hear. "Belknap?"

"Well, sir," Belknap says, "Mr. Stoughton and I recommend that we go back to using milled timbers and bolts for the rebuild. We can have the trestle disassembled and the men out of there by the time the construction materials arrive; maybe three or four days."

Mr. Adams moves Belknap aside to face the Vice-Chairman, "I agree with Mr. Belknap, Robert. We've wasted enough time and money trying to cut corners, not to mention the loss of life. Let's do this right."

Rake surveys the present state of the collapsed trestle, appearing unmoved by the sounds of suffering coming from the structure. After a moment in thought, he says, "All right. There are sawmills in Barre and Northfield. We can begin to get the milled timber we need here in a day or two so we can start the rebuild immediately. Getting the bolts may take a day or two longer." Turning to Treasurer Mazer, "Mr. Mazer, go with Stoughton to the store and have him tell you what he needs. We'll place our orders when we return south today." Turning to Adams, "Does that meet with your approval, Mr. Adams?"

Somewhat stunned by Rake's uncharacteristic acquiescence, Michael nods, but appears suspicious. Yet his only reply is, "Yes, that's fine."

Seeing Stoughton and Mazer haven't moved, Rake raises his voice, "Gentlemen, get going! Simon, go with Mr. Stoughton and get a list of materials." Rake turns to Michael, "Mr. Adams, please go with Belknap and Barnum and make certain we have plans in place to move forward." Mr. Adams hesitates, but follows Belknap and Barnum as they head toward the store.

Evidently, my invisibility must have been temporary because Mr. Rake seems taken aback and a bit annoyed that I have suddenly appeared in his field of vision. "And take him with you. He must be good for something." Rake pushes me in the direction of the other three men, and I rush to catch up.

Chapter 32

RAKE'S SOLUTION

Dismissed by Mr. Rake, I'm grateful to be only an annoyance and not seen as an extra mouth and a pair of hands the company could do without, so I trot off behind the two groups of men sent on their way by Rake. We hadn't taken more than a dozen steps when we hear a resonant "thunk" and the now familiar sound of cracking wood immediately followed by panicked shouts and the groans of men in renewed agony!

Barnum turns and is the first to speak, "My God! The trestle is coming down!" Everyone, every man and woman nearby, runs to the riverbank to watch in horror as the torrential flow of the river resumes its destruction, taking down most of what remains of the trestle and those trapped in it.

Men rush to the footbridge to recover whomever they can from the tangle of timbers, some flailing, others lifeless. Broken timber, wood, and flotsam are now piling up and firmly pinned against the footbridge by the relentless current crushing and drowning some of those who, for an instant, thought they were freed from the trestle's grip.

Above the shouting I hear Mr. O'Reilly just over my shoulder, "He did it! I saw him!" I turn to see Mr. O'Reilly running toward Rake and pointing to him with rage in his eyes, "He knocked out the support."

Just as O'Reilly is about to reach Mr. Rake, Sheriff Ferris steps between them. He has both of his rather substantial double barrel pistols drawn and pointed at O'Reilly's mid-section, "Stop right there, Mick."

O'Reilly is livid, pointing at Rake still holding the sledgehammer. "I saw him knock the support out. It's murder! That's what it is. It's murder! Arrest this man, Sheriff."

"Mr. Rake? Is that true?" asks the sheriff, holding O'Reilly at bay and glancing over his shoulder at the Vice-chairman.

"No, no, no, Sheriff. On the contrary. I noticed the support was slipping, and I was trying to secure it when it gave way. The ground and the wood are very slippery."

"He's lying, Sheriff. He hit the God damned support out from its place. He did it on purpose! I saw him!"

The sheriff turns his full attention to Patrick. He gets within inches of O'Reilly's face. Looking up at him, he puts one pistol directly under Mr. O'Reilly's chin while the other's muzzle remains pressed against Patrick's stomach.

"Look, Mick, I can believe you, or I can believe the honorable Vice-chairman of the railroad." Looking around at the audience that has gathered, the sheriff calls out, "Anyone here want to tell me that Mr. Rake is lying?" No one says a word. The sheriff continues, "Doesn't make sense that Mr. Rake would do further harm to his own trestle."

"Patrick!" Mr. Murphy takes Patrick's arm and turns him away from the sheriff and his firearms. "Come on, man."

Above the shouts coming from the river and general confusion of the moment, the sheriff says, "Oh, look who's here! It's Mrs. Dillon's suitor." The sheriff pursues Maury and Patrick as they walk away; Maury restraining Patrick from standing his ground. "Do you both want trouble? Because right now you're disturbing the peace."

Patrick turns to face his accuser, but with both hands against Patrick's chest Maury pushes Patrick backwards, forcing him to back-pedal, "Come on, Patrick, let's see what we can do to help."

Patrick replies, "I'll tell ya what we can do to help, we can take care of those bastards before they kill more of us!"

As Rake heads back to the train we hear Mr. Adams call out above the chaos, "Mr. Rake!" Barnum, Adams, and I rush to catch up to him. Mr. Adams steps in front of Rake, blocking his path. Rake steps to the side, but Mr. Adams moves with him, "What was that all about, Robert? What the hell did you do?"

"I don't owe you or anyone any more of an explanation." Rake pushes past Adams and continues making his way to the train. Yelling back over his shoulder to Mr. Adams, "Tell Belknap and Barker to come see me before we leave."

Barnum and I look at Mr. Adams who struggles to speak, "George, go tell Mr. Belknap and Mr. Barker to come see Mr. Rake in his car right away." Appearing to be in shock, Barnum manages a barely audible, "Yes, sir," and pushes into the swirling mass of people responding to the latest calamity.

Mr. Adams is immutably grim with anger. I'd seen his dander up in the boardroom, but I hadn't seen such rage in his eyes prior to this moment. His quick glance in my direction strikes me with so much force I stagger backwards. I continue my retreat and eagerly follow Barnum as he goes in search of Belknap and Barker. Looking back, I see Mr. Adams grab the handhold and swing himself up into the company's passenger car. Barnum heads to the store and pays no attention to me as he pushes through the crowd.

By design I fail to keep up, and, reversing my direction, I head back to hear what's going on in that railcar. I can hear raised voices as I draw near, and find a spot to sit with my back against one of the coach's iron wheels under an open window. Lucky saunters up from under the car, sniffs my hand looking for something to eat, I suppose, and lays down at my feet before letting out a sigh of resignation.

Mr. Adams is in mid-sentence, "...and that justifies sacrificing God knows how many lives just to save some time? Christ, man, what kind of moral standard is that?"

"I'll tell you once again, there are only two moral standards in business, Michael: the laws of competition limited only by the laws of man," says Rake, firm in his response.

"We shouldn't break the laws of the land and the Commandments of the Almighty just to beat the competition, Robert."

"The sheriff and the courts will determine if we broke any laws, and the laws of competition will condemn us to eternal failure if we don't do everything we can do to win the race with our rivals. You know damn well if we don't reach the Canadian markets first we'll be bankrupt. On the other hand, if we win the race we'll be rich, and our stockholders will be rich. We have no choice but to operate to the limits permissible. We have a moral duty to win the race."

Michael continues to press the question, "A moral duty? So you're saying we have a moral obligation to conduct our business according to the lowest permissible standard? We also have a moral obligation to God and mankind."

"Then let God be our judge!" says Rake. "In the meantime, we are operating under the same rules as our competitors. If there were rules that made us operate to a higher standard, and our competitors also had to live by those rules, then so be it. We'd be in a fair fight. But, until I hear God's verdict, we'll go by the same rules of commerce as our competitors. We've done no wrong."

"Bullshit," declares Michael. "We've shorted the payrolls, and our untested shortcuts have cost men's lives."

"We've broken no laws, Mr. Adams. Neither man's nor God's." Rake paused. "We haven't walked away from our debt to the workers; in fact, many of them are in debt to us. And, as far as the trestle design, we followed the standards recommended by a licensed engineer, and we are going to re-build having learned the new design needs improvement. That's progress! That's how we learn to do things better and faster and beat the competition. If someone thinks we have violated any laws, we'll defend ourselves and the company...in a court of law."

"You know damn well the only law in this valley is not going to take any action against you or our company." Michael's voice held a degree of resignation.

"Nor should he," counters Rake.

"But the trestle collapse…," Michael's voice regains a note of anger. "What the hell did you do, Robert?"

"You heard what I told the Sheriff, and I have nothing more to say; not to you, not to anyone. I only do what I think needs to be done for this company to succeed, and, God damn it, I'm going to see to it that we succeed!"

Belknap and Barker come running up to the railcar and don't seem to notice me or Lucky as they approach the steps into the car. "Mr. Rake?" calls Belknap.

"Come in, gentlemen," replies Rake. "Mr. Adams, I believe we are done."

The only reply I hear from Mr. Adams is, "I'll see what I can do for the men." The next thing I know, Mr. Adams jumps off of the railcar, pushing between Belknap and Barker, and heads toward the footbridge. Belknap and Barker climb the stairs to the car.

Lucky got up and follows Mr. Adams, so this seems like a good time for me to rejoin the camp. The scene at the river is familiar: rescuing whom we can, caring for the injured, and taking the twelve newly deceased to the back corner of the flats for burial in the morning.

Many hours later, I'm in the store when Belknap, Barker, and the three supervisors enter. "Gentlemen," begins Belknap. "We need to keep aware of what is going on out there. We don't want any more trouble."

Barker is looking for direction, "How do you want to see the next day or two play out, Henry?"

"We'll let the men hold the funerals tomorrow morning. We won't have any new building supplies for a day or two, but we need to keep them busy. There's clean-up to do, but let's not push them," says Belknap. "Frankly, I'm worn out, and the men are, too. I suggest we all go back to the hotel tonight, get a good night's sleep, and come back here tomorrow afternoon after they conduct their funeral service and take their noon meal. We'll muster the men, assure them Mr. Rake has approved returning to the standard construction method, and get set up for the next push."

Belknap continues, "For the remainder of the day I want you all to help with the injured, and be sure to spread the word that we will be using the old tried and true methods for trestle construction when we start to re-build. And for God's sake, stop any talk about what caused the collapse. It was an accident, plain and simple. Don't get into any arguments, but take the names of anyone who gives you trouble. Any questions?" The men look at one another, but no one says a word.

Turning to Barnum, "George, you and I should pay a visit to the gent who accused Mr. Rake of knocking out the support. Do you know where to find him?" asks Belknap.

"Yes, sir, that's Patrick O'Reilly. I know where he's camped," says Barnum.

"You and I should go have a talk with Mr. O'Reilly when things calm down a bit. Meet me back here before supper, and you can take me to his tent." Looking at the other men, "If there's nothing else, then go out and look and listen to what's going on." No one moves. Belknap looks puzzled. "Well, is there anything else?" Several of the men look at each other, and each mutters, "No."

As everyone is making his way to the door, it opens and Sheriff Ferris appears, standing aside to let everyone pass.

"Mr. Belknap," says Ferris. "Can I have a word with you, sir?"

"What is it, Sheriff?"

"I just want to confirm that all of the twelve dead were immigrant workers, and their deaths were the result of the bridge collapse. You know, no foul play."

"Yes, Sheriff, that's what happened. I have a list of their names right here…"

"No, no, that won't be necessary," says the sheriff dismissively. "We have no record of those men being here, so there's no reason to file any official record of their deaths. Say, if you need more help, I can send word up to Montreal and Quebec…."

Belknap impatiently cuts him off, "No need, Sheriff. Now if you'll excuse me, is there anything else I can do for you?"

"No, sir. My work here is done, so I'll be headed back before it gets dark, or, maybe you'd like me to stay in case of more trouble," says Ferris.

"That won't be necessary," says Belknap shooing the sheriff away with a flip of his hand. The sheriff tips his hat and leaves the store. After a moment, Belknap follows him out.

I finish my chores inside, and make myself useful the rest of the day bringing drinking water around and lending a hand when needed. As usual the conversations don't stop when I'm near, but as soon as a supervisor gets near men stop talking. Their talk is all about the miserable living conditions, little or no pay, and now what appears to be the railroad's disregard for life and limb. The general mood is dark, and there is anger and resentment building with an intensity I haven't heard before. As the day wears on the spirit of our makeshift community seems to have collapsed right along with the trestle. The muted wails of mourning echo throughout the valley into the evening.

As suppertime nears I'm carrying a bucket of drinking water and ladle following Belknap and Barnum as they weave their way through the tents to O'Reilly's campsite. Mr. O'Reilly is standing outside his tent talking with Mr. Murphy and two other workers. The two workers leave when they see us approach.

"Mr. O'Reilly, can we have a word with you?" asks Belknap. O'Reilly doesn't say anything, but standing up straight he faces Belknap with his arms across his chest.

"In private, Mr. O'Reilly?"

"Mr. Murphy can hear whatever you have to say, Mr. Belknap," says O'Reilly, standing his ground.

"Whatever you think you saw happen this morning is over and done. The sheriff is satisfied no wrongdoing took place, and I just want to make certain we can put this all behind us. I'm here to ask you not to cause any more trouble, or I'm going to have to ask you to leave the camp." Belknap is firm in his delivery.

Hearing Mr. Belknap's threat, Mrs. O'Reilly emerges from the their tent and stands next to her husband. "Patrick, listen to what the man says." Patrick scowls as he looks at his wife, but his expression softens when he sees the genuine concern in her pleading eyes.

Patrick turns slowly back to Belknap, "Yes, sir. I understand."

"Very well then." Belknap needs to say more. "I want you to know that we're going to rebuild the trestle using the standard methods and materials. No more shortcuts. We have the supplies we'll need on order, and they should be here in a day or two. In the meantime, we are doing all we can for the injured, and those who perished will have a proper burial tomorrow. We are very sorry for what has happened, and we're going to do all we can to see that it doesn't happen again."

As Belknap turns to leave, Patrick, touches his arm, "What will happen to the widows and their children?"

Belknap looks at the ground and takes a moment to consider his answer. He looks back up at Patrick, "We'll settle their accounts and provide transportation to the nearest settlement." Belknap adds as he starts to walk away, "That's all I can promise." Mr. O'Reilly watches Belknap's back recede into the failing light.

Patrick turns to Mr. Murphy, "God damn it! That's not doing enough. At least the Brits would have extended some kind of aid to a grieving widow."

I walk up to the three with a ladle outstretched. "Now Patrick, swearing won't help the situation," says his wife. "You can do more good for you and I by not causing any trouble. I'm afraid of what will happen if they see you as a troublemaker."

"And I'm afraid of what will continue to happen if nothing changes," replies Patrick.

No one takes the ladle I'm offering. In fact, I don't think anyone is even aware I am here, so I hold the ladle up in front of Mr. Murphy. Upon seeing the ladle magically appear, he takes the ladle mouthing an exaggerated, "Thank you," as he takes a drink. "Patrick," begins Mr. Murphy, "Let's keep talking to the other men. I think nearly all of them agree we can't continue on this way."

Chapter 33

LIFE AFTER DEATH

After supper, the camp is quiet, and even Catherine's tavern is deserted. Groups of three or four workers come together briefly around a campfire, exchange words, and then go off in different directions and coalesce with another small group, and so on. The supervisors do their best to keep up with the flow, but each small group comes together and breaks up before their conversations can be overheard.

In the fading daylight I see the shadow of Mr. Murphy cross the footbridge toward Catherine's, and he disappears behind the boardinghouse. Not able to suppress my curiosity, I make my way across intending to imbibe a wee bit, if necessary, so I can keep tabs on what's happening. When I get to the tavern door and open it, I can see no lanterns are lit, and no one is inside. What can I do to get close to whatever is happening in the back? Nothing comes to mind, and moreover, I begin to feel like I'm intruding and out of place. So I withdraw back across the bridge and find Lucky asleep in front of the store. I sit down next to him, exhausted and ten feet short of my cot inside. Leaning against the outside wall, I fall asleep, too.

Come dawn, but well before sunrise, Mrs. Dillon's rooster wakes me in time to see Mr. Murphy again walking across the footbridge toward the boardinghouse. It's none of my business where he spent the majority of the night, but this time he's carrying what seem to be two full valises, one at the end of each arm. Catherine comes out to meet him and gives him a kiss on his cheek. A few minutes later, he reappears from behind the boardinghouse empty handed, but accompanied by his daughter who gives him a hug. Catherine comes out and stands next to the Christine and watches as Mr. Murphy makes his way back to the camps. When Mr. Murphy is across the bridge, he turns and waves.

Gray smoke from the campfires hangs over the valley in the still morning air. The only sound is the muffled clang and scrape of spoons on metal plates. There is no conversation to be heard. The two priests who are members of the crew are scurrying from tent to tent, pausing at each cluster of men, announcing the funeral service will begin shortly. I've begun the clean-up from breakfast when I hear a hand bell ring. Likely, it's one of the priests using it to call the workers and their families to the funeral service.

I quickly finish my duties and join the tail end of the procession to the far corner of the Flats. The hand bell rings continuously until all are gathered. I can barely hear the priest conducting the service, but its cadence is familiar, and it takes all of my concentration not to participate out loud in the responsive portion. Toward the end of the service, our resident fiddler plays a mournful dirge. Hearing it brings tears to my eyes that I could not hold back, and my tears are not the only ones being shed this morning. To end the service, the priest breaks from tradition and speaks the words from a hymn that's been around since the States' Revolutionary War, and is still heard in taverns and schoolhouses throughout New England:

Let tyrants shake their iron rods,
And slavery clank its falling chains.
We fear them not, we trust in God.
New England's God forever reigns!

The priest recites the last line in full throat, and a spirited "Amen!" comes from the congregation. All assembled immediately begin a hurried trek back to their tents, passing around me as if I were a rock in a rushing mountain stream. What is going on? Something is unfamiliar. The atmosphere is not one of mourning, but one full of purpose. I can't remember a time when there wasn't at least one supervisor on site, but none are here this morning. Is that the difference?

Men and women are grim and determined as they disappear into their tents only to emerge shortly carrying packs and bags and duffels.

On Bolton Flats

People traverse the side paths among the tents and join together with others on the main paths leading to the footbridge. Only after a vast majority of the camps' inhabitants have gathered by the river does any one voice rise above the others, and that voice belongs to Mr. O'Reilly who calls out, "Today, all we seek is justice, and justice we will have!"

A great "hoorah!" comes from the crowd, and the first in line start across the footbridge, and onto the Stage Road. Even some of the injured, bloodied bandages and splints worn like badges of honor, join the procession. On the other side of the river, Catherine and Christine are standing in front of the tavern, satchels at their feet. Catherine waves as Mr. Murphy makes his way across just behind Mr. O'Reilly. She and Christine pick up their bags and join him and the rest of the march heading west to Jonesville.

Lucky comes and sits by my side seemingly full of as much wonder as I. We watch spellbound as all of this transpires until Lucky could hold back no longer. He takes several excited steps toward the footbridge, turns to look at me with what appears to be a smile on his face, and then takes several more steps, as if to say, "Come on, Doug, this looks like fun!" Of course, it isn't likely to be fun for the workers or for the supervisors, but this mongrel and his human counterpart at least have to be witnesses to whatever is transpiring. On the other hand, do I have a duty to run up ahead and warn the supervisors? No. No… I'm deaf, I seldom utter more than a grunt, and most of the time I'm invisible.

Lucky runs up ahead, tongue out and tail wagging, but I think it best for me to stay back and not march with the camp. Better to maintain my distance from the workers as I have all season. A few of the women and children and those who are too injured to walk stay behind. All who are able stand by the river waving to those marching across the river and west up the Stage Road. I let the tail end of the parade get almost out of sight before I start to follow, and I keep them in sight for all of the five miles to Jonesville.

As I approach the town I see the entire camp has encircled the hotel which stands where the road up from Huntington meets the stage road. As I get closer I can hear someone giving a speech about throwing off the chains of Tyranny. Across the street from the hotel, Catherine,

Christine, and Blacksmith Strong stand in front of the wide open barn doors of Mr. Strong's shop watching the spectacle.

From an upper window of the hotel Belknap and Barker are leaning out to see what is going on and who's speaking, but the speaker is on the porch of the hotel and cannot be seen from above. They withdraw their heads, and a few minutes later Belknap opens the front door of the hotel and walks out on the porch. He is greeted with a collective and disdainful "boo".

Belknap addresses the congregation, "I understand you have grievances, but they will not be settled by this kind of demonstration. I suggest you all return to the camp, and…" He is interrupted by Mr. O'Reilly who had been speaking, and O'Reilly raises his voice for all to hear as he addresses the project manager. "Mr. Belknap, we will not be returning to camp, and you and your men, sir, will not be leaving this hotel until we have received our full wages. Give us our pay, and we will disperse – this is all we ask and this we will have!"

Mr. O'Reilly and several other men force Belknap back into the hotel as shouts of "Here, here" and "That's right!" come from the crowd. Other voices, one on top of another, defiantly join in until someone starts a verse and a round of a well-known British protest, "The Diggers Song":

The Gentry must come down,
And the poor shall wear the crown.
Stand up now, Diggers all!

Neither Mr. Belknap or any other supervisor is seen nor heard from for the rest of the morning while the fiery speeches of rebellion and songs of protest continue. Just past midday, Mr. Barker emerges and motions Mr. O'Reilly to come into the hotel, but Patrick goes no farther than the front door. The crowd is relatively quiet except for an occasional, "Hey, what are you saying?" coming from the rear of the crowd. Finally, Barker withdraws, and Patrick thrusts his arm in the air as he addresses the crowd, "They have asked that we let one of them go to Burlington to retrieve payroll!"

A great cheer rises up as Mr. Barker sheepishly sticks his head out the door and cautiously steps off the porch. The workers part, making a path to the blacksmith's where the contractors' horses are liveried. A few minutes later we all watch as Barker exits Mr. Strong's stable, already mounted, and rides off at full gallop to the west, leaving behind a cloud of dust. The apparent victory invigorates the gathering and infuses the speeches with renewed righteousness, and songs are sung with more conviction.

Burlington is some fifteen miles west, maybe a bit more, down the Stage Road, and, although Mr. Barker is likely to reach there this afternoon, it is not likely he will be returning today. But why would he go to Burlington? The company's primary accounts in Vermont are in Northfield some thirty miles in the other direction. I wander over to the blacksmith's shop where Mr. Murphy is standing with his daughter and Catherine. Lucky is curled up in Mr. Strong's open doorway lying in the afternoon sun. Mr. Murphy wears a puzzled glance when Catherine greets me with a smile and says, "Hello, Doug," out loud. I can see she is saying "hello" so I smile as I tip my hat with a half bow from the waist and turn to watch the show across the road.

The entire assemblage appears to be well organized. A small cadre of men canvass the crowd to see who would be "at station" during the night to prevent any other railroad supervisor from leaving, and others pass word that blacksmith Strong has agreed to provide sleeping quarters in his loft.

Word must have spread to nearby farmers that a crowd is afoot in town because several appear approaching from Huntington with carts and buckboards carrying greens, root crops, and preserves they are offering for sale. There are just a few customers for their goods until Catherine approaches several of the local farmers, dispenses a number of bills and coins from her purse to each, and the astonished men empty their wagons before driving off.

From my observation, this whole event has taken on a carnival atmosphere. Children are playing outside the wall of workers encircling the hotel, guarding the front and back doors, while men give speeches and the whole of the gathering occasionally breaks into song. The food

Catherine has purchased is spread out in front of the blacksmith shop across from the hotel, and people are taking just what they need, some leaving money in place of the goods they take. Actually, all is quite orderly.

I decide the best strategy for me is to stay outside of the hotel and yet remain apart from the protesters as well. I find a perch on the hitching post in front of Mr. Strong's shop, occasionally wandering inside just out of curiosity. At his anvil, concentrating on forging rims for a set of wagon wheels, Mr. Strong pays little attention to me. I see that his coal bin needs to be restocked, so I bring in several bucket loads, each received with a smile and a nod. Perhaps it is in return for my industry that he lets me explore the premises and use his privy while others have to find other accommodations.

Mr. Strong's establishment, opposite the hotel, is quite large. His blacksmith's shop is well equipped, and off to the south side is a stable and barn with a loft. His living quarters appear to be in the rear, although I haven't gone in there, and he has another shop at the north end of the building where there are several wagons and farm implements in various stages of repair. Connecting the repair shop to the main shop are small two rooms: one holds blacksmithing supplies with a window that faces the street, and the other room is empty, except for a large table against one wall, and a door that opens to his main shop and forge.

While Mr. Murphy and O'Reilly are preoccupied with the protest, Catherine and Christine are inseparable. I see Lucky follow them as they wander off hand in hand toward the Stage Road and around the corner in the direction of the general store. Quite a while later they return; a new bonnet atop Christine. Although her face is shaded by the brim I can see she is grinning from ear to ear. I watch Christine move from here to there until Mr. Strong notices her new hat. To Christine's delight, Mr. Strong pauses from his work and compliments her on it. I laugh out loud when the following thought occurs to me: Surely the best part of having a new hat is to have someone notice it!

I hear Mr. Strong offer his private quarters to Catherine and Christine for the night since he thinks it best for him to remain in his shop, considering all the activity going on just outside.

The afternoon gives way to dusk, and as night falls there are more songs than speeches with an occasional prayer thrown in for good measure. The number surrounding the hotel diminishes only slightly as some women and the younger children make their way to the blacksmith's loft for the night. Christine and Catherine socialize with some of the other women and children for what must have been an hour or two past sunset. I don't see them after that.

I intend to stay up all night, but the protesters have a system that allows a dozen or so men at a time to catch a few hours sleep and then be awakened by the protesters they will replace on station at the hotel. As the night wears on I find it difficult to keep my eyes open, so I, too, manage to catch a few hours sleep after finding a very nice carriage in Mr. Strong's repair shop in which to recline comfortably.

Chapter 34

INDEPENDENCE DAY

Perhaps it is just a coincidence that today is July 4th, the 70th anniversary of the United States' Day of Independence; the day this great country declared its independence from Great Britain. Rather than being premeditated, it certainly appears the unanticipated events surrounding the trestle collapse, and not the calendar, instigated this insurrection. But God works in mysterious ways, and it does seem right and fitting these new refugees from the famine and British demagoguery are here on this day defying unjust authority and protesting their oppression. Would it also not be fitting if today Mr. Barker returns with the payroll, and this insurrection results in justice for these men? Yes, it would be fitting indeed!

Since I have no role in the protest, nor one serving the supervisors being held captive in the hotel, I make myself useful assisting Mr. Strong. Lucky, too, chooses to spend most of his waking hours wandering around the blacksmith's shop. I replenish the coal to feed the forge, pump the bellows, and bring iron from the supply room to be formed into wagon wheel rims, horseshoes, and so on. I rather like the work, and Mr. Strong smiles and nods as he continues pounding the hot iron without breaking his pace to do the menial and mundane tasks I am now performing.

This second day of protest is much like the first. At dawn the supervisors plead to be released assuring the men supervisor Barker will be returning soon, but the men hold their ground and refuse to free them. Other guests are allowed to come and go, some amused by the spectacle, others supportive, and still others contemptuous of the workers' defiance. The speeches continue to assert their demand for fair treatment and draw frequent parallels with the oppression they suffered under the Brits and thought they had escaped. Indeed, it does seem the only difference is the Lords of America are Lords born of commerce rather than Lords born of bloodline, but from the laborers' perspective the result is the same.

I'm quite happy to resume my role as Mr. Strong's helper, and as I am retrieving stock from his supplies, not much more than an hour after sunrise, maybe two, I can hear through the open window one of the men stationed as a lookout on the Stage Road announcing that a rider is coming from the west, causing a great cheer to arise. The speaker stops in mid-sentence in anticipation of Mr. Barker coming 'round the corner, but instead, there is only the sound of horses and wagons growing ominously louder and louder until finally the lookout comes running back, "An armed force is coming, an armed force is coming!!"

Patrick takes to the porch and urges all to hold their ground, but the women scoop up the children and head for Mr. Strong's barn.

The first to appear is Sheriff Ferris at full gallop, with a pistol drawn and held aloft, closely followed by Marshall White and an armed contingent of Burlington's Light Infantry in full uniform. They appear to be bolstered by a several score of armed volunteers. The unexpected sight of an armed force making such a dramatic entrance alarms the workers, many of whom flee. Lucky comes running into the stockroom barking and excited, so I drop to my knees and hold on to him, with a hand around his muzzle to stop him from giving away our hiding place, thinking it is in my best interest not to be seen as aligned with the workers. On my knees and peeking out the window I can see Mr. Strong's instinct is to head into the fray.

The sheriff and U.S. Marshall part the few remaining workers as they ride directly up to the porch and dismount where Mr. O'Reilly and others are standing defiantly. Several armed members of the infantry also dismount and stand directly in front of the porch with their long guns pointed at Mr. O'Reilly, Mr. Murphy, and the several of the other men remaining on the porch. The sheriff and the Marshall ascend the stairs of the porch holding what appear to be shackles and leg irons. "Marshall," says the sheriff standing within a foot of O'Reilly, "Arrest these men for sedition against the peace of the State of Vermont and Chittenden County."

"Gentlemen," begins Marshall White turning partially toward the men in front of the hotel and holding the shackles aloft, "It will be my duty by the power vested in me by the Congress of the United States of America to arrest you for inciting insurrection if you do not disperse immediately." Upon hearing the Marshall's threat the men who haven't already fled start toward the barn. It's then Mr. Strong steps up on the porch, and he, Mr. O'Reilly, and the Marshall engage in what appears to be a heated discussion.

Ferris, looking around and apparently satisfied that his work is done jumps from the porch and… shit! He's headed our direction. Dropping to the floor and still holding onto Lucky, I'm thinking I just need to be invisible a little while longer and then leave with the supervisors when the ruckus is over. I can manage that. But less than a minute passes when I hear the door to the outer room open and the clank of chains. To my horror I hear the sheriff bark, "Get in there. Both of you." My God! Whatever is happening is going on in the next room.

I hear Catherine say, "You can't hold us, Sheriff, and don't point that gun at me. We've done nothing wrong."

"Certainly you have, Mrs. Dillon!" says the sheriff. "Everyone knows you smuggle your liquor in from Canada and pay off whoever it takes to get away with it. Now you're going to pay me off, and this girl is going to watch or I'll have to kill you both while resisting arrest."

"I know you!" says Christine. "You're the man I saw running from my schoolhouse the day Mrs. Flanagan died. You're the man who hurt Mrs. Flanagan!"

"Why you little bastard," says the sheriff. "Yeah, that was me, because your teacher wouldn't….she wouldn't cooperate."

I can't believe my ears! Dear God, what can I do? Lucky, upon hearing Christine's voice, tears from my arm and rushes into the other room. I hear a gun discharge and a whelp from Lucky, so without thinking I leap to my feet and burst into the room. Lucky, still barking, is crouched on the floor in front of the sheriff who has both of his pistols drawn; one now pointed at me and the other at Catherine. Christine is kneeling next to Lucky.

"Well, look who's here. I've got three rounds left, and there are three of you, so…"

Before he could finish his sentence - or execute our sentence, the shop door opens and Marshall White enters with his pistol drawn, and Mr. Murphy and Mr. Strong are right behind him. "What's going on here, Sheriff?" Mr. Murphy went over to his daughter.

Surprised and fumbling for words, Ferris says, "Marshall, I was, uh, arresting this woman when the dog attacked me."

"That's a lie!" says Christine looking at the Marshall and then her father.

"Don't listen to her, Marshall," says Ferris. "She'll say anything to protect Mrs. Dillon."

"The sheriff killed my schoolteacher!" says Christine. "I saw him running from the schoolhouse." Turning to her father, "Remember when that happened, Father?"

"Is that true, Sheriff?" the Marshall asks.

"No. Of course it's not true. I don't…"

"It is true," I say. "I heard him confess to the crime just before you got here, Marshall."

Everyone is dumbfounded at hearing me speak. The sheriff is shocked most of all. He turns toward the Marshall with both his pistols drawn, and BANG! A single shot rings out. The sheriff drops his pistols and clutches his belly as he drops to the floor face down.

Catherine knees and embraces Christine. Slowly, all eyes turn toward me. The Marshall walks over and towers over me. "Who are you, and what did you hear?"

Excited, and suddenly released from my yearlong silence, I say, "I work for Mr. Belknap and the railroad supervisors. I was in the storeroom when the sheriff came in and threatened to harm these two women. When Christine said she recognized Ferris as the man who killed her schoolteacher, he confessed and said he was going to kill them both. That's when Lucky ran in and the sheriff shot the poor thing. He threatened to kill me, too!"

Mr. Murphy rolls the sheriff onto his back. "He's dead, Marshall."

"Mr. Murphy," orders the Marshall, "Get some help to carry him out to a wagon. I have other matters to attend to." Turning his attention to me and Catherine he adds, "Don't either of you leave the county. I'll need your statements."

Catherine walks over to where I'm now standing and gives me a hug and a kiss on my cheek. "Thank you, Doug. I think Lucky will be all right. It looks like the shot just grazed him."

Having heard the second gunshot a few men had gathered in the open door to the shop; Mr. O'Reilly among them. The Marshall, addressing the group, returns his gaze to Mr. O'Reilly.

"Gentlemen, I'll give you one more warning. If you do not disperse peacefully within the hour, I will arrest anyone who does not have legitimate business here in town."

Realizing the futility of their continued resistance, the rest of the men head to the barn to retrieve their belongings and loved ones to begin their trek west on the Stage Road.

Seeing the men disband and hearing no retort, the Marshall leaves the shop and walks over to the militia and others gathered in front of the hotel, including the railroad supervisors who had finally been allowed to leave the hotel.

O'Reilly came inside the shop. "Maury, what the hell happened here?"

"Evidently, the sheriff was a murderer, and when he turned his gun on the Marshall, the Marshall shot him. Everyone seems all right." Says Maury. "You heard the Marshall. What are you going to do, Pat?"

"The way I see it we don't have much choice, but I'm not going back to the camp and neither are most of the men. Kathleen and I talked about it. We're going to go on to the Winooski's mills, and see what work I can find there," says Mr. O'Reilly extending his hand toward Mr. Murphy who clasped it in both hands.

"You did the right thing, Patrick," says Mr. Murphy. "God knows how many more of us would have died this season."

"What are you going to do, Maury?" asks Patrick.

175

Maury turns and smiles seeing Catherine standing with her arm around Christine. "Well, we talked last night, and for now Christine and I are going to return with Catherine to help her run the boarding-house.

Chapter 35

THE DUST SETTLES

When the supervisors learned that I had duped them for more than a year, they wanted no part of me, and more than a month after the insurrection work on Bolton Flats still hasn't resumed. So, Mr. Strong was nice enough to offer me a job in his shop as his helper and apprentice. Lucky mended quickly and divides his time between here with me in Jonesville and back with Catherine at her boardinghouse across from the now abandoned worksite.

Travelers on the Stage Road sustain Catherine's business, and Mr. Strong and I like to make the trip to spend an evening every now and then at the nearly empty tavern. When I do visit Catherine's, Lucky occasionally jumps on my wagon to accompany me back to Jonesville. I made a nice home for myself in the blacksmith's room where all of the action took place on Independence Day, and the sheriff's blood still stains the floor. For my labor I get the room and two dollars a week, plus I'm learning a new trade. Maybe I'll look for a teaching job one of these days, but right now I'm just grateful to have landed safely after all the turmoil of this past construction season. I'm sure as hell never going to work for the railroad again.

Our insurrection caused quite a stir among the locals, and the write-up in the Burlington newspaper got the story right. In fact, the editor seemed to be sympathetic to our plight, writing that we, the workers, were not the first wrong-doers. The paper placed that blame on the railroad for committing the sin of benefiting from the workers' uncompensated labor. Imagine that! Could it be this country will not tolerate injustice?

The story about Christine recognizing the sheriff gets re-told at the tavern every now and then. Mr. Murphy tells the story like this: When Christine was about eight years old, she had forgotten her chalkboard and returned to her school after class to retrieve it. As she approached the building, she heard her teacher, Mrs. Flanagan, crying for help. But before she could reach the building, a man ran out the side door and disappeared into the woods. Inside, she found her teacher on the floor of the school, her dress torn and a feed sack over her head. Mrs. Flanagan had been assaulted and beaten, and died shortly thereafter from her injuries. Christine was too young to know all that Mrs. Flanagan had suffered. When the local Constable questioned Christine, she said she didn't recognize the man who ran, so the Constable concluded he wasn't a local man, and he was never caught.

Oh, and as for Mr. Murphy and Christine, Catherine invited them to stay with her, for how long, I don't know. It seems Christine is still in charge of the chickens and learning frontier life, and Mr. Murphy... well, I'm sure Mr. Murphy is making himself useful as the new man of the house. There's much work to do in the warm months before winter sets in here in the North Woods: getting in firewood, putting up hay, and so on. And, as in the past, Catherine continues to board travelers and is already starting to plan for next year's construction season, having made an offer on some property closer to Jonesville.

In the meantime we have several months before snow falls in earnest, and the trip to Catherine's boardinghouse is still pleasant. In fact, Mr. Strong and I are thinking that tonight would be a good night to pay a visit to Catherine's. August in these hills can be hot and humid, and today is no exception. Working anywhere near that forge on a hot day gives a man a thirst well before noon and lasting the rest of the day.

When Mr. Strong said we were done for the day, we both jumped into the Onion River running along the south side of his property to cool off, then set off in his buckboard to spend the evening in Catherine's company. With the summer coming to an end and the workers dispersed, the only people to patronize the tavern are the few of us who live nearby and travelers on the Stage Road. Catherine always lets the drivers of the coaches that pass by eat and drink free of charge, so just about every coach stops and lets the passengers find refreshment. Catherine is some business woman!

It's still odd to return to the construction site. The few workers that returned to work after the insurrection packed up the campsite and then were sent on their way never receiving all the wages they were owed. Remnants of the collapsed trestle are still in the river, and the white-washed crosses marking seventeen graves at the far corner of the Flats can be seen from the Tavern. But the positive spirit in the air within the tavern's walls is infectious, and there's always good conversation laced with laughter, accompanying the excellent spirits available by the glass!

As the early evening light fades, the Flats are illuminated by a full moon rising in the east. Inside, Mr. Murphy, Catherine, and Christine are at a table playing a card game called Reverse using a fine set of Catherine's varnished playing cards. Tonight there are no customers other than Mr. Strong and me. Mr. Strong goes behind the bar and brings out a checkerboard, and he and I play checkers for most of the evening. It's a pleasant way to pass the time, and since we all know each other so well, the talk and banter is unguarded. Eventually, Christine heads upstairs to her bedroom above the kitchen.

Among the small talk, I can't help but hear Catherine say to Maury, "I am so happy that you and Christine came into my life." Reaching out and putting one hand on Maury's arm, "Christine is such a special young lady."

Mr. Murphy replies, "I'm grateful for the love you have shown to her, Catherine, and she and I appreciate the special feeling that comes from being a family."

"That feeling is only going to get stronger," says Catherine, a twinkle in her eye.

I still have the ability, after a year of practice, to be occupied with one activity or another and yet able to listen to every word within hearing distance. Perhaps that is why Catherine says she had something to tell Mr. Murphy and asks him to join her in the backroom.

"Gentlemen, we will return shortly," she says as she takes Maury's hand and leads him into the kitchen. Several minutes pass before the two reappear, and Mr. Murphy goes behind the bar. Reaching down, he stands up with three cigars in his hand and says, "Gentlemen, I'm going to be a father!"

POSTSCRIPT: FOR THE RECORD

- Burlington Free Press, July 11, 1846 - "Disturbances on the Railroad"
- Excerpts from Personal letters – July 1846
- Mrs. Dillon's Obituary, January 11, 1872
- Vermont Central Railroad Board of Directors and Officers, 1846-47

Years ago this author heard of an incident referred to as "The Bolton War," said to be Vermont's first significant labor strike. But little was known about the event, and only a paragraph or two about the Bolton War appeared in Vermont history books at that time. The basic arc of the story as told in the main text is true, but the author added several characters and events beyond the known history. Presented below are the facts from the best sources available, most of which were found in the collection of the Vermont Historical Society's Vermont History Library located in Barre, Vermont.

In the late winter of 1846, the Vermont Central Railroad recruited out of Canada approximately two hundred Irish immigrant men and their families fleeing the Great Potato Famine to lay approximately five miles of track through Bolton Flats during the coming eight month construction season. Although the Burlington newspaper reported "16 to 18" of the 200 workers were killed in the several months prior to the insurrection, the author could find no historical record of the precise number who perished or the causes of their deaths. The railroad did construct a trestle just east and up river of Bolton Flats, but there is no indication building a trestle was a part of the 1846 construction season for the Bolton crew.

The names of the some of the supervisors and the sheriff are taken from public records. Personal correspondence found in the Vermont Historical Society collections, included below, describes the events of that spring and summer. Although the record indicates Sheriff Ferris was more cooperative with the railroad than sympathetic to the workers, his crime and demise in this story are fictitious.

The workers did cease work and hold supervisor Barker prisoner in his hotel, demanding the pay they had not received for their work. They also stopped all passage on the stage road using "violent language" and digging a trench across the road according to the following "Burlington Free Press" account.

From the Burlington Free Press, July 11, 1846:
Disturbances on the Railroad

Considerable excitement was aroused in our town on Friday last, by the sudden requisition of the Sheriff, Mr. Ferris, for an armed force to aid him in the execution of legal process, which had been forcibly resisted by the laborers on the Central Railroad, near Richmond in this County. The principal facts in the case, as we learn them from the Sheriff, are these:

On Friday morning last, information was communicated to the Sheriff, by Mr. Deputy Gleason of Richmond, that the laborers on the Railroad, (some 200 in number.) about three miles east of Huntington's tavern, had suspended work, and collected together, were engaged in disturbing the peace in various ways — that they had thrown implements in the way of the mail stages running between Burlington and Montpelier — and with violent language and demeanor had attempted completely to prevent the free use and occupation of the road by the public — and finally they were holding in duress Mr. Barker, one of the principal Contractors, peremptorily refusing to liberate him.

The Sheriff promptly repaired to the scene of the outrages accompanied by two of his deputies and Mr. Church, Constable of Burlington, and by peaceful means endeavored to cause the rioters to disperse. – His Proclamation to the (unintelligible) disregarded, and his attempt to release Mr. Barker forcibly and successfully resisted. Obtaining the necessary warrant for the arrest of the supposed ring-leaders, he again encountered resistance, and the individuals arrested were rescued by force from his custody.

Under these circumstances the requisition of an armed force, above alluded to was promptly resorted to by the Sheriff – The Light Infantry Co. in Burlington were called out, and the Company of Firemen immediately and unanimously tendered their services to maintain the supremacy of the law, and were furnished by the Sheriff with arms and ammunition.

With this force, amounting to seventy-five or eighty men, the Sheriff again reached Richmond, on Friday evening accompanied also by a number of our most respectable citizens. On Saturday morning, either intimidated by the presence of an armed body of men, or otherwise awakened to a conviction of the fruitlessness, as well as the criminality, of further resistance, the Disturbers had mostly dispersed. Mr. Barker was released, some ten or twelve were arrested and lodged in jail in Burlington, and thus the affair terminated – fortunately without bloodshed or further outrage.

One word regarding the cause of this disturbance, and we leave the topic. It appears that the grounds of complaining on the part of the laborers was that they were not paid for their labor, & that they received no pay for several weeks. Their language to the Sheriff was, "give us our pay and we will disperse – this is all we ask and this we will have." Now these were poor men, earning their daily bread by the sweat of their faces, and they ought to have been promptly paid. Holding all resistance to the laws, and all illegal combinations for the purpose of redressing even real wrongs, in utter abhorrence, and believing that they should be suppressed, promptly and, if necessary by armed force, we yet unhesitatingly affirm that the laborers, indefensible as their conduct became, were not the first wrongdoers. That sin must lie at the doors of those who, knowing their necessities, continued to receive the benefit of their un-rewarded labor.

We know how easily these sentiments may be misconstrued and misrepresented, But we cannot help that. Those who, by injustice, incite others to a violation of the laws of the land, should and will, in the estimation of good men and merciful judges share the responsibility of the crime, however unequal may be the legal allotment of punishment. "Be just and fear not" is an admirable maxim but Be just and you will have nothing to fear is a much more practical truth.

We understand that those who employed these men are Messrs. Smith & Co., subcontractors in the 4ᵗʰ remote. The Directors of the Company will undoubtedly take such steps as will be likely, hereafter, to prevent irresponsible men from having it in their power to involve the community in difficulty and danger by unjustly withholding from the laborer his hire.

Excerpt from Personal letters – July 1846

From Edward Jones of Richmond, Vermont, to Milo Jones, Fort Atkinson, Wisconsin Territory, dated July 7, 1846, just as it was written:

…The Irishmen on the Rail Road about Ransoms and up in Bolton have had a Row. Their employers did not pay them. They Rose in mass took one of the Contractors and kept him in duress, dug a ditch across the Road and Stoped the stage 2 or 3 hours, make a mark across the Road and tell Teamsters not to pass on perill of their lives. Lawyers and judges Came from Burlington to purswade them to take a different Cause, but all to no purpose. Ransom for ten days hired a gard to protect himself and Buildings. This State of things want to be Endured.

Two companies of militia were call out, and when the Pats see them they fled to the mountains in Bolton to save their bacon, however they succeeded in taking 9 of the leaders and they are now Confined in jail in Burlington. The rest I understand are leaving the place as fast as possible, so you see the war is Ended and peace and quiet is Restored. I can't give further particulars as all this took place while I was gone and I have not seen Ransom since my Return…

Four days later, Mr. Jones wrote the following to Jabez Jones, Esquire, Westchester County, NY, dated July 11, 1846:

….But, recently the R.R. chaps have had a break up in some way or for some Cause they did not pay their workmen and the Pats waged a small

mexican war. Shut up one of their directors stopped Teams on the Road, forbid them to pass, dug ditches across the Road and stopped the stage two hours before they Could pass. Their employers ought to have paid them but this state of things Could not be endured. The militia were called out and when the Pats saw them Coming they fled to the mountains in Bolton. They succeeded in taking 9 and confined them in jail and this week they have been trying them. I was at Burlington Wednesday, one had been tried and Cleared. I think they will make this state some $3000 Expense. The Corporation ought to pay it. The R.R. to me seems to be a rather uphill business. Years must pass away before it is completed.

The General Contractor for the Vermont Central Railroad, Sewall F. Belknap, eventually defaulted on his contract, and construction was completed in later years by other contractors. Former Vermont Governor Charles Paine, President of the VCRR, was personally brought to financial ruin as well because of the failed construction season. He later joined the Board of Directors of the Vermont & Canada Railroad that completed the laying of track to the Canadian border in 1864. The Central Vermont Railroad rose from the ashes of the VCRR and eventually competed laying track through the Winooski Valley to Burlington.

Mrs. Dillon's Obituary

Catherine Driscoll Dillon was a real character who immigrated to the United States in her late teens. She and her husband ran a succession of successful boardinghouses where "whiskey was always available" and followed the construction of the railroad all the way to Rouses Point on the New York side of Lake Champlain. She procured her inventory mostly by smuggling due to the high taxes on the importation and sale of liquor. Catherine did indeed extricate herself from her marriage in the manner described in this story, however, her scheme was executed successfully years later during the U.S. Civil War. This is her obituary as printed in the "Burlington Free Press" on January 11, 1872:

Catherine Driscoll Dillon was a very remarkable woman, and no one had obtained a greater notoriety. She came from Ireland a poor and young woman, with her husband about the time of the building of the Vermont Central and Vermont & Canada railroads in the 1840's. She kept a boarding-house for the laborers along the line of the road, and she would relocate her business each season as the railroad construction crews progressed up the Winooski River valley west to Rouses Point on the shore of Lake Champlain.

At her boarding-house whiskey was always available to her boarders and others, in spite of the efforts of the contractors. After the railroads were completed, she moved from Rouses Point to St. Albans, and continued in the same occupation.

About the time the "Maine Law" was first enacted, and for years afterwards, she continued to make life lively for the police forces. Catherine herself, as well as others whom she would hire, brought the contraband to the States. Though difficult to capture, she was arrested scores of times, and as often escaped either from the county jail or from the courts of justice.

Some suspect that Catherine had well-developed relationships with those responsible for enforcing the laws and benefited from their assistance. In 1867 she was indicted by the United States District Court for being connected with smuggling and for trafficking in smuggled liquors. She was convicted and obliged to submit to a fine of $2000 which she paid.

During the time of the Civil War Catherine had become tired of her husband. It is important to remember that Catherine had befriended many railroad workers over the years and perhaps knew every railroad worker by name. She obtained a divorce from her husband, it is claimed, in the following manner:

Mr. and Mrs. Dillon were returning from a trip on the cars when Mr. Dillon failed to find his valise among the baggage on the platform. On Catherine's advice he selected another bag from those in the pile of baggage for the purpose of exchanging the bag for his when his was found. No sooner had they reached home than she procured his arrest for larceny. The unfortunate man was sentenced to Windsor prison, and as a condition of his release, went out in the Vermont Cavalry Regiment as a bugler.

In one way or another Catherine amassed a considerable fortune, variously estimated at fifty to seventy-five thousand dollars. In her younger years she was considered handsome, but later her personal beauty had become somewhat failed, owing to the excessive use of stimulants. At her death she was about forty-five years of age.

Vermont Central Railroad Board of Directors, 1846-47

Charles Paine, Northfield, Vermont
Robert G. Shaw, Boston, Massachusetts
Samual S. Lewis, Boston, Massachusetts
Jacob Forester, Charlestown, Massachusetts
Daniel White, Charlestown, Massachusetts
John Peck, Burlington, Vermont
Lucius B. Peck, Montpelier, Vermont

VCRR Officers 1846-47

Charles Paine, President, Northfield, Vermont
Samual H. Walley, Treasurer, 17½ Tremont Row, Boston
E. P. Walton, Jr., Clerk, Montpelier, Vermont

ABOUT THE AUTHOR

The author was inspired to research "The Bolton War" when he was assembling lesson plans to support the teaching of labor history in Vermont schools and colleges. Finding only passing references in available textbooks, he spent many days combing through the records and ephemera kept by the Vermont Historical Society to uncover details of the event.

Peter has held a variety of positions in human resources management and labor relations in Vermont and Massachusetts, including Personnel Officer of the Vermont Highway Department, research analyst for the Vermont Higher Education Planning Commission in the Vermont Governor's Office of Budget and Management, and director of the Labor Management Cooperation Program for the City of Burlington, Vermont. Peter also served as Chief Negotiator for the Vermont State Employees Association, Director of the Vermont Federation of Teachers and Health Professionals, AFT/AFL-CIO, and president of the Vermont Labor History Society.

Made in the USA
Charleston, SC
17 January 2014